BRAD WILLIAMS

DEMON STONE

First published by Darkenwilde Publishing 2024

This novel is entirely a work of fiction. The names, characters and incidents portrayed in it are the work of the author's imagination. Any resemblance to actual persons, living or dead, events or localities is entirely coincidental.

First edition

ISBN (print): 978-1-991343-19-2
ISBN (digital): 978-1-991343-28-4

This book was professionally typeset on Reedsy.
Find out more at reedsy.com

Contents

Prologue

The Wasteland Druid stood atop a crumbling ridge, his cloak of woven desert vines fluttering in the unrelenting wind. His eternal gaze swept across the Forbidden Wastes, where the dunes writhed like serpents beneath a crimson sky. He had seen this land devour the unwary and swallow empires whole, its secrets buried under sandstorms that tore flesh from bone. Yet tonight, the Druid sensed something different, a stirring in the threads of fate.

The winds whispered names - Aidan, Ahlissa, Jillian - and the desert carried their echoes like ancient hymns. He listened, his gnarled staff planted firmly in the shifting sand. The voices of the Wastes told him of a scholar, a captain, and a freedom fighter, bound together by purpose and tragedy. They sought answers in a land where questions were dangerous, answers more so, and the cost of knowledge could be as steep as eternity itself.

The Druid's empty eye sockets burned with a green magical energy, his mind drifting with the whispers. Through the Wastes, he had watched countless wanderers rise and fall. He knew the signs of those marked for something greater - or something darker. The desert had claimed kings and beggars alike, yet these three carried the weight of the past and the light of a precarious future.

The winds howled, whispering of a man named Aidan. The Druid envisioned him; a slender figure moving with purpose, his golden eyes sharp and searching. He was no warrior by nature, but the desert had a way of tempering steel where once there had been only flesh.

Aidan was haunted by nightmarish visions, the Druid knew, though he had not spoken of them to many. The desert had shown him fragments of a city buried deep beneath its sands; Qualtesh, a name the Druid had not heard in centuries. It was a place of sorrow and power, where the light of the Kale Ashtari had been consumed by shadow.

The Druid had seen many like Aidan over the years, drawn by whispers of forgotten history and promises of greatness. Most came seeking treasure or power, only to find death. But Aidan was different. He bore the mark; a sigil burned into his flesh, pulsing with the essence of Dark Aethyr. The Druid recognised its shape, a deviant pattern tied to the demon Izen'draazt.

The demon's name lingered in the wind like a curse, and the Druid's staff tightened beneath his grip. The scholars of Kanarzand had unleashed horrors in their thirst for knowledge, but few bore the scars of that folly so deeply as Aidan. His path was dangerous, not just for himself, but for all who followed him.

The winds shifted, bringing the scent of distant rain; a lie, the Druid knew, for no rain fell here. Still, the scent carried with it another name: Ahlissa.

The Druid pictured her standing proud on the deck of her airship, Zephyr Breeze. Her silver blonde hair gleamed like the sun against the desert's eternal twilight, and her eyes held the sharp clarity of a seasoned leader. She was pragmatic, but the Druid had seen the cracks in that armour.

Ahlissa carried her own ghosts, though she would never show them to her crew.

She was a captain who had carved her name into the annals of Scylla's most daring explorers. While others sought only survival, she sought understanding, unearthing ruins and delving into the mysteries of their ancestors. The Druid respected her tenacity, even as he pitied her ignorance. The past she sought could not be uncovered without consequence.

The desert had claimed greater leaders than Ahlissa, yet she defied it, sailing its skies like a bird refusing to fall. Her strength had kept Aidan alive thus far, but the Druid wondered how long even her resolve could hold against the darkness rising around them.

The wind softened, almost tender now, carrying the faintest whisper of Jillian. The Druid felt the shift, the way the sands seemed to sigh at her name. She was of the Khystar, a people who clung to light even as shadows tore their sanctuary apart.

The Druid could see her clearly, even from this distance - her lavender gold-flecked eyes burning with defiance, her flowing red-gold hair a banner against despair. Jillian followed The Path of the Light, a faith her ancestors had kept alive despite the encroaching darkness of The Aspiring Dream.

The Druid had no love for the Sah'ren - parasitic entities that twisted their hosts into soulless zealots. He had seen their corruption first-hand, how they whispered sweet lies to the desperate and turned them into weapons. Jillian bore the weight of their destruction, her heart a cauldron of grief and fury.

3

Her light burned brightly, but even the brightest flames could be extinguished. The Druid knew that better than anyone. He had seen the strongest of wills break beneath the weight of despair. Yet something in Jillian's spirit made him pause. She was a spark the Sah'ren could not extinguish, no matter how they tried.

The Druid's vision continued as the wind howled again, louder now, more insistent. The sands shifted beneath him, revealing fragments of bone and obsidian, relics of those who had come before. The desert was speaking, telling him that Qualtesh awaited these three.

The city of the Kale Ashtari lay buried deep, its ruins a testament to a once-great people consumed by darkness. It was a place of sorrow and power, where the Demon Stone pulsed with the remnants of Izen'draazt's influence. Had remained forgotten for centuries. But now, the sands whispered of a new chapter unfolding.

Aidan, Ahlissa, and Jillian were drawn together by threads of fate the Druid could not fully see. Their journey was not theirs alone; it was part of a story written long before their births. The sands had chosen them, and the desert would test them.

The Druid shifted his staff, its tip sinking into the sand. He would watch their journey, as he had watched countless others. He would listen to the winds and see what secrets the Wastes revealed.

The desert did not give freely, but it did give. And those who survived its trials emerged stronger, though rarely unscarred.

In the distance, he imagined the Zephyr Breeze cutting through the sky, its sails taut against the rising storm. He imagined Aidan studying his visions, Ahlissa steering her ship with steady hands, and Jillian sharpening her blades in silence.

The desert would test them. The darkness would tempt them. But the light they carried might yet endure.

The Druid turned away, his cloak billowing in the wind. The Forbidden Wastes had seen empires rise and fall, but it had not yet seen the likes of these three. And for the first time in centuries, the Wasteland Druid allowed himself a sliver of hope for Scylla's future.

1

The Pursuit

Ahlissa paced the wooden deck of her prized airship, The Zephyr Breeze, her boots tapping against the polished planks as she scanned the horizon. Her first mate, a tall and perceptive Argar named Jalik, approached swiftly from the helm, his face shadowed with concern.

"Captain," he said, his voice barely above a whisper but tense enough to command attention. "Two airships are trailing us. They appeared shortly after we left the city limits."

Ahlissa squinted, shielding her eyes against the glare of the afternoon sun as she followed his gaze toward the rear. Two small, nimble airships were indeed on their tail, hovering just above the tree line and matching the Zephyr Breeze's course with disturbing precision. They followed along the rugged coastline, never too close but just within sight.

"Can you make out their markings?" she asked, her voice a study in cool composure.

Jalik took a long, assessing look. "Yes, Captain. Their sails bear the dark raven emblem of House Mhorvaeus. From Sindarr."

Ahlissa's eyes narrowed. House Mhorvaeus was known for its ruthless mercantile ventures and uncanny knack for information gathering. For some time, rumours had reached her that Lord Mhorvaeus himself had expressed a keen interest in her airship, even sending envoys to inquire about its speed, engineering, and armaments. But she'd never expected such a brazen act.

"Well, this is interesting," she murmured with a faint smirk. "Impressive, really. I didn't think Mhorvaeus would drop all pretence of subtlety just to make it so painfully obvious that he wanted to follow me."

Ahlissa tilted her head thoughtfully, signalling for Jalik to bring her spyglass. She raised the polished lens to her eye, zooming in on the tailing airships. The Mhorvaeus insignia was unmistakable, a raven's wing marked in black against crimson sails. Her amusement waned, replaced by a wary resolve.

"Take us further out to sea," she ordered finally, lowering the spyglass. "I don't want them lurking in our shadow. Increase our speed just enough to break visual contact."

Jalik nodded, barking orders to the crew, who adjusted the flight surfaces and coaxed the powerful vessel to accelerate smoothly over the shimmering water of Iron Bay. Within minutes, the trailing airships fell back, gradually swallowed by the haze of distance until even the last faint outline of their hulls vanished.

As the waters far beneath them deepened from the turquoise of the coast to the endless dark blue of open sea, Ahlissa exhaled, allowing herself a moment of relief. Yet her mind raced. There was a high probability that Mhorvaeus' ships had been recently acquired; after all, she'd had no reports of House Mhorvaeus using such swift models before. They were test vessels, she concluded, sent to probe her airship's capabilities, to measure her response.

"They must be new acquisitions," she said, almost to herself, watching the horizon as if the answer might appear out of the mist. "Perhaps Mhorvaeus was only testing their speed against ours. It's no secret he's shown... a particular interest in the Zephyr Breeze's unique design."

Jalik, still at her side, shifted uncomfortably, his gaze scanning the empty sky. "Credit where it's due, Captain; Mhorvaeus certainly knows how to make his intentions clear. He wants us to know he's watching."

Ahlissa gave a single, humourless chuckle. "Indeed. But there's something more at play here."

The first mate raised an eyebrow. "More, Captain?"

Ahlissa nodded. "Think about it. Why would Mhorvaeus go through all this trouble to tail us on what appears to be a routine trade mission?" She tapped her chin, her brow furrowing. "Our real mission remains secret. On paper, we're delivering standard supplies between Gideon City and Kharadia, as far as anyone in the city knows."

Jalik glanced at her with a cautious expression. "Captain, do you think... perhaps he's privy to our true mission?"

Ahlissa's gaze grew distant, her mind flashing back to the whispers she'd heard from her contacts about Mhorvaeus' recent dealings.

Her thoughts drifted to an encounter with an unusual ally, Baron Von-Claagen, a figure cloaked in mystery and known for dabbling in forbidden knowledge. The Baron had been particularly interested in the Dark Aethyr Crystal, an artefact rumoured to hold the remnants of an ancient power.

Before she could voice her suspicions, Jalik spoke again, his voice low and tense. "Given what I overheard Mhorvaeus discussing in the shadows of the Sindarri Embassy, and after our last encounter with the Baron... I think there may be a connection between the two."

Ahlissa's eyes widened in realization. "Are you suggesting Mhorvaeus intends to avenge the Baron's fall? That he believes we've taken something of immense value from him?"

Jalik's face darkened, and he nodded. "Precisely. What if it wasn't just the Baron acting alone in his pursuits? What if Mhorvaeus funded the expedition in secret? There was something unsettling about both men."

"The undead tongue..." Ahlissa whispered, the words slipping unbidden from her lips.

Jalik nodded, understanding immediately. "That's it. The Baron spoke it fluently, as did Mhorvaeus. It's not a language one encounters often, Captain. In fact, it's rarely heard outside the darkest halls of Sindarri necromancers."

A chill ran down Ahlissa's spine as she recalled the tone, the inflection, the unsettling cadence of the words she'd overheard. The memories of Von-Claagen and Mhorvaeus murmuring that same ancient dialect - their voices almost identical in their sinuous flow, their pronunciation

9

eerily precise - played back in her mind.

"It wasn't just that they spoke the language," Jalik continued, voice steady and unnervingly calm. "It was the way they spoke it. There was an unnatural fluency there, something I can only describe as... otherworldly."

Ahlissa's hand moved instinctively to her belt, where a small, encrypted communicator lay concealed within the folds of her cloak. She withdrew it, glancing at Jalik with a stern nod. "I'm sending an urgent message to the Aystaran Embassy in Gideon City," she said, her tone brokering no argument. "And I want all my contacts within The Machination on high alert. If Mhorvaeus is indeed plotting against us, we need to understand his motives and uncover any links he might have to other powerful parties."

Her fingers moved deftly over the communicator's interface, her message brief but packed with encoded information. The Aystaran Embassy had long been an ally of her family, their ancient alliances woven into the political fabric of their houses. They would have eyes and ears in places Ahlissa herself could never hope to reach.

As the message pulsed away, signalling its delivery, Jalik took a step closer, his eyes filled with a troubled intensity. "Captain," he said quietly, "I stand by my instincts. Mhorvaeus and the Baron... they are not normal men. I felt it with both of them, just as I felt it when I met Lord Khannay. It's like... they carry a darkness within them, a presence I cannot explain. An aura beyond mere power or influence."

Ahlissa met his gaze, her own filled with resolve. "And thus far, Jalik, your intuition has proven as valuable as any intelligence network."

She sighed, a weight settling on her shoulders as she turned to look at the open sea, its vastness somehow both comforting and ominous. "From this point onward, we assume Mhorvaeus is watching us. Every step, every turn. I want double watches posted, and I want any unusual sightings reported directly to me."

As the hours passed and the Zephyr Breeze sailed further into open waters, Ahlissa couldn't shake the feeling that they were being toyed with, manipulated by unseen forces pulling strings from the shadows. She was no stranger to intrigue and power plays; the world of airship trade and political manoeuvring was fraught with such dangers. But this; this was different.

She could sense Mhorvaeus' presence lingering like a cold shadow, a silent threat lurking just beyond her reach. The man was notorious for his ambitions, his willingness to cross lines others dared not. Rumours abounded that he had delved into necromancy, forging alliances with spirits and creatures most people only encountered in their nightmares. Some even whispered that his mastery over life and death had extended to himself, that he had achieved a state beyond mortality, existing in some ethereal limbo.

As night fell, Ahlissa retired to her cabin, though sleep eluded her. She reviewed the past months in her mind, retracing every step, every interaction that could have possibly drawn Mhorvaeus' attention. From her dealings in the bustling city of Gideon to her clandestine meetings with The Sceptre Guilds, each decision seemed to have led her one step closer to this shadowy game of cat and mouse.

When dawn broke, she emerged onto the deck, her resolve hardened. Whatever Mhorvaeus and his mysterious associates were planning, she would not be caught unprepared. Standing at the bow of the ship, she whispered a silent vow to herself and her crew. She would unmask Mhorvaeus' plans, uncover his secrets, and defend the mission she'd been entrusted with, no matter the cost.

It was then that a voice from behind startled her out of her thoughts. Jalik, looking as haggard as she felt, spoke with a quiet intensity. "Captain... we've received a response from the Aystaran Embassy."

He handed her the small parchment, and as she read, her face grew solemn. The embassy had confirmed her worst suspicions. Mhorvaeus was indeed allied with forces beyond Sindarr, his connections rooted in a shadowy web that spanned realms she'd only heard about in whispers. And, chillingly, the Baron's interests were somehow tied to an ancient artefact they believed was now on board the Zephyr Breeze.

Ahlissa met Jalik's gaze, the two of them bound in an unspoken understanding. They were far from alone in these waters. And while the journey ahead promised danger at every turn, Ahlissa knew she would face it with unwavering resolve.

"Tell the crew to prepare," she said, voice steely. "If Mhorvaeus and his allies want a game, then we'll give them one they'll never forget."

2

The View from the Deck

The waters of Iron Bay stretched in vast expanses of blue green, shimmering gently under a calm sky. It was a rare, windless day, and the slight breeze barely disturbed the placid surface of the water, fanning small waves that sparkled under the morning sun. Above, the airship Zephyr Breeze maintained a steady altitude of about a hundred feet over the bay, cruising smoothly and at a steady acceleration. It was a serene flight - ideal conditions for sailing, as Ahlissa often remarked - and the crew appeared in high spirits.

Aidan, aboard the deck, inhaled the freshness of the air, letting the briny scent fill his lungs. He found the experience of open-air flight utterly exhilarating, an unbridled freedom he seldom enjoyed. Today, with no pressing duties, he moved freely about the deck, taking in the beauty of the ocean and the clear sky above. He saw Jillian at the observation post on the port side, partially sheltered by the ship's overhang. She stood alongside two Kale Khestari soldiers, her face animated with laughter, her usual solemn demeanour softened by light-hearted conversation. Aidan couldn't help but smile at the sight; even in their challenging line of work, small moments like this reminded him of the joy and camaraderie that kept their spirits afloat.

Yet, Aidan's task that day demanded his attention, and he eventually made his way to the interior of the ship where the Dark Aethyr Shard lay secured under heavy guard. He checked on the shard periodically, noting its pulse-like glow, a faint light that seemed to emanate from within, casting eerie shadows around it. Every so often, Aidan conferred with the team of scribes and scholars tasked with deciphering the shard's mysterious inscriptions. Unfortunately, their efforts had reached a temporary impasse; the texts and symbols defied all straightforward interpretation, each line leading them deeper into obscure meanings and tangled historical references. Frustration grew among the team as progress slowed to a halt.

The shard itself, however, seemed to affect Aidan in ways he couldn't explain. When in its presence, he felt a peculiar compulsion; a magnetic pull that tingled at the back of his mind, seeping into his thoughts. He had come to dread the sensation, yet it drew him closer, whispering fragments of unknown language he couldn't consciously translate. He had taken to asking others if they felt anything similar, but each time, his inquiries were met with polite, quizzical smiles and polite shakes of the head. None of the scholars, guards, or even his closest companions seemed affected in any way. It was as if the shard singled him out, plucking at his senses while leaving others untouched.

More disturbingly, Aidan had begun to hear faint, muffled voices, distorted and warped as if echoing from an endless corridor. The language he heard was ancient and peculiar, a blend of dialects from across races and centuries, a hybrid tongue that eluded complete understanding. Aidan suspected the voices aligned with the runes on the shard - a mix of arcane symbols he had painstakingly begun to translate. But the meaning remained elusive, jumbled and fragmented, as though the shard's messages were trapped between realms, communicating from a world just beyond the reach of the living.

On some days, Aidan found himself overcome by a sudden, inexplicable urge to instruct the scholars to leave the room. "You've worked hard. Take a break. Rest up," he would say, almost as if compelled by another force to usher them away. The scholars, though puzzled, had learned not to question him and would quietly comply. Aidan himself couldn't shake the feeling that something was urging him to be alone with the shard, to indulge in an unguarded interaction that might yield secrets otherwise hidden.

Uneasy with his growing obsession, Aidan sought out Ahlissa, who was speaking with Jillian on the upper deck. With their trust and rapport, he knew Ahlissa would listen without judgment, perhaps even offer insight he hadn't considered. He requested that she and the head scholar join him in a secure, private meeting below deck, away from the crew's ears. Ahlissa agreed immediately, arranging for two loyal crew members to guard the door.

Inside the dimly lit chamber, Aidan looked to Ahlissa, Jillian, and the head scholar. He hesitated, words catching in his throat as he wrestled with how best to explain his predicament. Finally, he spoke.

"Ahlissa, you know me well," he began, a strained tone betraying his unease. "I think... something is happening to me when I'm near the shard. I don't understand it, but it feels as though it's speaking to me, or trying to. And I feel compelled to listen, to act in ways that don't feel... entirely my own."

Ahlissa's brows knitted in concern. "How do you mean, Aidan?" she asked, her voice calm but searching.

Aidan turned to the head scholar, hoping he could substantiate his experience. "How many times," Aidan asked, "have I told you and your team to leave the room when I come near the shard?"

The scholar considered the question before replying. "At least five times, perhaps more," he answered thoughtfully.

Aidan nodded, grimly satisfied with the response. "Each time, I asked if you felt what I was feeling, if any of you heard... the voices, or felt the compulsion. You all looked at me as if I were speaking nonsense. It's clear that none of you experience this, but I can't ignore it any more. The last language we deciphered matches some of what I'm hearing. It's fragmented, confusing; but there are voices, and they are addressing me. I feel... summoned."

Jillian's gaze sharpened, her expression one of suspicion. "You think the shard is aware of you, actively communicating?"

Aidan's lips pressed into a thin line as he grappled with his answer. "Yes. I know it sounds strange, but it's as if the shard recognises me. I believe my past encounter at the Star Haunt - when I met the guardian of the Kale Ashtari - may have something to do with it. Perhaps it marked me in some way."

Ahlissa leaned forward, her expression thoughtful. "What exactly are you proposing?"

Aidan took a deep breath. "I want to enter the room alone and engage with the shard without any mental barriers or distractions. I've resisted this connection for as long as I can, but I believe that if I allow myself to experience it fully, we might uncover valuable knowledge. The shard wants to reach its destination, and we're its means of transportation. I don't think it will harm us. But if I can understand its message, we may gain insights critical to our journey; especially if we're venturing into the Forbidden Wastes."

The head scholar regarded him with a wary frown, casting a sidelong look at Ahlissa, who then turned to Jillian. Jillian hesitated, and after a long moment, she addressed Aidan directly.

"Aidan, we've all observed the way you respond to the shard," she began, her tone almost clinical. "It's an intense focus, bordering on obsession. You're the only one affected in this way. We believe it may be exercising a kind of mental domination over you. I've spoken with Ahlissa about it, and... it feels similar to what my people know as possession by the Sah'ren - a spirit force from The Aspiring Dream."

Aidan listened in silence, a faint glint of defiance in his eyes. "I know, Jillian. I've confided in you about the distraction it creates. But if there's a chance this could help us understand what we're dealing with, then we have to take the risk. You can lock me in chains afterward if you're worried, but at the very least, consult with your elders for guidance."

Ahlissa considered his plea, her gaze far away as she weighed the possibilities. After a long pause, she gave a nod. "I think the representative would indeed welcome an audience with you. He has knowledge beyond our comprehension and may be able to guide us."

Aidan blinked, taken aback. "I wasn't expecting to meet him myself, but... if you think it wise, I'll go."

Ahlissa placed a reassuring hand on his shoulder. "Remember, Aidan, this representative is ancient, one of our living ancestors. Though he walks between life and death, he is a force of wisdom and guidance. Just be yourself. Speak honestly and heed his counsel."

3

The Representative

The corridor that led to the representative Athovhar's guest quarters was both austere and foreboding. Dimly lit sconces cast shadows along the stone walls, and the air grew perceptibly colder the closer Aidan came to the Deathless One's quarters. Even those unfamiliar with Athovhar's presence sensed the chill in the air; a coldness not of mere temperature, but a pervasive, ancient energy that seemed to drain warmth from the very atmosphere.

Four of Ahlissa's trusted guards, clad in dark armour with insignias of her house, stood at attention outside the plain wooden door leading to the representative's quarters. These guards had been trained to offer unwavering loyalty and an almost reverent respect for the Deathless One, an entity both venerated and feared among their people.

Aidan approached, pulling his cloak tighter against the creeping chill. The guards recognised him instantly, inclining their heads in silent acknowledgment.

"The representative wishes to see me," he said, his voice steady but laced with curiosity and a hint of apprehension.

With a nod, the guards stepped aside, and Aidan moved past them, feeling the weight of their watchful gazes as he approached the door. Once he entered, the door closed behind him, and he found himself in a small, dimly lit chamber. Heavy, dark curtains shrouded the windows, casting the room in shadows. Only a few candles illuminated the space, their faint flickering light reflecting off tapestries that hinted at an ancient Aystaran history.

At the centre of the room, seated in a high-backed chair adorned with silver inlays, was Athovhar, the Deathless One. Cloaked in magnificent robes of deep blue and silver, Athovhar's figure seemed to shimmer as if cloaked in layers of illusion. His face, though unmistakably Aystaran, was enigmatic; piercing sapphire eyes shone from beneath a cascade of grey hair, and his stature, even seated, was imposing. Aidan felt as though he were in the presence of a being far older and wiser than the centuries his appearance suggested.

"Welcome, Aidan of Kanarzand and of the Aystar," Athovhar intoned, his voice a hauntingly resonant sound that seemed to bypass the ears and echo directly within Aidan's mind. "I am most pleased to make your acquaintance. I have heard much of you."

Aidan hesitated, struck momentarily by Athovhar's presence. His voice, though laced with hesitation, emerged firm. "I have not seen one of your kind before. But I know of you and understand the reverence Ahlissa, and her people hold for you."

Athovhar chuckled softly, his laugh as gentle as it was unsettling.

"And I, in turn, have not encountered one quite like you. You bear the appearance of an ordinary half-Aystar man, yet there is more beneath the surface. I sense it; a difference, a spark. Your journey intrigues me, and your quest brings you into contact with forces that pique my interest. In truth, I am here not merely for knowledge but to observe. The High Aystaran Council received word from the ambassador in Gideon City of your progress, and I have come to witness it myself. What do you think of that?"

Aidan shifted, absorbing Athovhar's words with a mixture of surprise and satisfaction. "I am honoured and... somewhat taken aback," he admitted. "For what I have learned suggests that those who call themselves the Khestar once mingled with your people, Athovhar. I suspect there is more to our Aystar heritage than most are aware."

Athovhar's sapphire eyes gleamed as he considered Aidan's words. "An interesting notion," he mused, his voice low and reflective. "The history of the Aystar is long and often shrouded in mystery. As you may know, we began as a race enslaved by giants; beings who ruled in the wake of the world's destruction by demonic forces. Those demons had inherited the world after a cosmic clash between primordial shadowy entities and evil creatures in the Age of Darkness. But we, the deathless... we have grown curious, questioning our origins and the lost knowledge of those early days. That is where you, Aidan, have a role to play."

The weight of Athovhar's words hung heavily in the air, and Aidan felt as though he were on the brink of understanding something far greater than himself. The representative's gaze pierced him as he continued, "I have heard of your struggles, the path you walked in Kanarzand, and your search for belonging. You have spent time with your kin, the Kale Khestari, and glimpsed the dark legacies that haunt our heritage. Tell me, is it true that you encountered a being at the Star Haunt, one who recognised you as kin?"

Aidan nodded slowly, summoning the memory of his strange encounter. "Yes. At the Star Haunt, I confronted a guardian... a corrupted creature who sensed my bloodline. It allowed me passage because I bore the same heritage as those who had created it. In a hidden chamber, I witnessed a vision of ancient Aystar; powerful, regal, yet tainted by a darkness they willingly embraced. These were no ordinary Aystar; they wielded corruption as a weapon, knowingly risking its toll on their own spirits. I learned that they did not originate here but journeyed from another world. Before departing, they left traces of their blood among the Aystar of this world. I believe... they seeded a legacy that survives to this day. I learnt their name is Kale Ashtari."

Athovhar listened in silence, his expression unreadable but intensely focused. "Fascinating," he murmured. "And I sense your search for knowledge has led you to the shard, a stone of immense power and ancient lineage. Tell me, Aidan, what compels you to heed its call?"

Aidan took a deep breath. "The shard's presence is unlike anything I've known. When I am near it, I feel a compulsion; a pull that is as powerful as it is unsettling. It speaks to me in languages we've only recently deciphered, though the messages are fragmented and unclear. At times, I find myself driven to send others away, to be alone with it. I believe it wants to communicate, and I feel as though it may hold answers to questions I haven't yet asked. My intention is to let it speak, to allow it to reveal what it desires."

Athovhar's face darkened, his gaze sharpening. "You may not fully understand, but the shard has already claimed a measure of control over you. It calls to you not as a guide, but as a master. You are carrying it toward its ultimate destination, and whether you intend to or not, it is guiding your path. I cannot interfere with this bond, nor sever it. The stone will compel you until it reaches its place of origin, and only then will you be free. I have seen this in prophecy, Aidan. This is why I, Athovhar, have joined this expedition; to bear witness to its fulfilment."

Aidan's mouth went dry at Athovhar's pronouncement, yet he found his resolve undiminished. "I am aware of its influence, but I do not believe I am powerless. The shard may have its own agenda, but I retain my sense of purpose. I believe I can balance my will against its compulsion. By understanding what it wishes to communicate, we may yet learn something invaluable. There are lives at stake, Athovhar, and I cannot turn away from this burden. If engaging with the shard's voice will aid our cause, then I must take that risk."

Athovhar observed Aidan in silence for a long moment, his gaze penetrating. At last, he inclined his head. "Then so it shall be. Pursue this path but know that the Kale Khestari blood within you will be tested. They were warriors, driven by conquest and pride. They abandoned Kharadia for lands they won through war, and their pride became their legacy. I sense traces of them in you, though your spirit seems... gentler. In time, this duality will reveal its own challenges, as will the shard."

Aidan considered Athovhar's words, taking comfort in his understanding. "Are you suggesting that others, like the Kale Ashtari, will recognise this connection? That my heritage may draw their interest?"

Athovhar's eyes gleamed with a dark wisdom. "The Kale Ashtari and the Kale Khestari are branches of the same ancient tree, split by cataclysmic events. When the Kale Ashtari were forced underground, they forged a life in darkness and became something different, though their essence remains rooted in the Khestar. The shard, I suspect, is guiding you toward remnants of this shared heritage; a place where evidence of their history lies. That is why you must proceed. The answers you seek will only be found by following its call."

The implications of Athovhar's words sent a chill through Aidan. "It seems the shard grows darker the deeper we delve. I fear there may be a presence within it, something waiting to be unleashed."

"Perhaps," Athovhar replied, his tone grave. "The shard serves many purposes, some of which may be beyond our understanding. It will reveal a past not all Aystar will accept, truths that might challenge their identity. Yet it must return to its place of origin to release something... or someone. What that has remained obscured by prophecy."

Aidan's mind raced, his thoughts tangled with the possibilities Athovhar had suggested. "And how does this connect with the ancient prophecies of the Keepers of the Past?"

Athovhar shook his head slowly. "Prophecies are as fragmented as the world's history. Each race holds a piece of the truth, but none possess the entire tapestry. We must be patient, Aidan, for only time will reveal the full story. I, myself, have waited two thousand years to witness this unfold."

The weight of Athovhar's words settled over Aidan like a mantle, and he felt his purpose crystallize. "The shard, in many ways, is a key; a relic that transcends boundaries between races and eras. I sense a universal connection, as if all languages and all histories trace back to a single source. Perhaps the shard wishes to reveal that truth to us."

A faint, knowing smile crossed Athovhar's face. "Precisely. I have lived long, but to be present at the uncovering of such truths... this, Aidan, is why I joined this journey. To finally see history converge, even in part, is a gift that few deathless may witness."

Aidan rose, offering a respectful nod of gratitude. "Thank you, Athovhar. Your insights have strengthened my resolve."

The Deathless One inclined his head. "Be well, young Aidan of the Kale Khestari. Seek the truth with courage, and we shall see what destiny unfolds."

As Aidan left the chamber, he found Ahlissa and Jillian waiting in the main corridor. Aidan's face was contemplative, and they noticed a new gravity in his expression.

"Ahlissa," he said quietly, "that meeting was... remarkable. Athovhar shared his name and revealed that he has waited two millennia for this."

Ahlissa's eyes softened with respect. "Our ancestors are bound to us through time. Did he offer guidance regarding the shard?"

"Yes," Aidan replied. "He believes the shard is leading us to a place where ancient knowledge waits to be revealed. It may relate to the Kale Ashtari, who were Khestar before their descent. This revelation may unsettle some, but he did not discourage my intent."

"Then we will make the necessary preparations," Ahlissa said firmly. "Your path is clear, Aidan. Let us see where it leads."

4

Cordovar

The Zephyr Breeze glided through the sky, descending toward the coastal city of Cordovar as the sun dipped below the horizon, casting a warm, amber glow over the land. The city stretched out along the coast, its skyline a blend of elegant towers, spires, and domed buildings built from stone that glistened faintly under the fading light. Narrow canals threaded through Cordovar's bustling heart, giving the city an intricate, almost labyrinthine appearance from the air.

Aidan stood at the bow, watching as the city grew larger, its lights flickering to life in anticipation of dusk. Ahlissa joined him, her face illuminated in the dimming light, a faint but knowing smile on her lips.

"Cordovar's a place of many faces," she remarked, glancing at Aidan. "It thrives on trade and secrets. Here, information is as much a commodity as gold."

Aidan turned to her, his curiosity piqued. "Is that why you suggested coming here?"

Ahlissa nodded. "Precisely. There's someone here you should speak to; a man named Matax. He's... well, let's just say he's knowledgeable about the kind of history you're seeking, the origins of certain bloodlines, and other matters others consider best left forgotten."

"Matax," Aidan repeated, storing the name. "And how do I find him?"

Ahlissa's eyes gleamed. "He operates out of an apothecary on the eastern side of the city, not far from the Grand Market. Just mention my name, and he'll know you're trustworthy."

As the ship descended lower, Aidan felt a faint knot of tension in his stomach. Cordovar was unfamiliar territory, a place where hidden forces wove their own agendas. He glanced over to Jillian, who stood nearby, watching him with concern.

"Aidan," she said softly, "I know that look. You're planning to do this on your own, aren't you?"

He offered her a small, reassuring smile. "Yes, Jillian. This is something I need to handle alone. The fewer people involved, the better. I don't want to attract unnecessary attention."

Jillian crossed her arms, eyeing him with a mixture of frustration and understanding. "Just... be careful. Cordovar isn't forgiving to strangers who dig too deep."

"Why is that?" he enquired.

"Cordovar is regarded by many as a paradise, the most peaceful city in all of Scylla. But it is a fact that its people have little tolerance for violence or unrest," she warned. "Few visitors to Cordovar realise there is a secret police force operating in this city and that it can administer strict justice without impunity or fear or reprisal. We know them as The Trust."

Aidan looked alarmed. "How do they operate?"

Jillian looked at him directly, with a serious expression on her face. "They employ many spies and assassins. Their primary concern is any matter that will affect the peace, stability and security of the nation. Any perceived threat is stamped out, efficiently and quietly."

The Zephyr Breeze touched down on the outskirts of Cordovar's main airship port, where dock hands rushed forward to secure the ropes and secure the vessel. As the crew began their tasks of securing the ship, Aidan gave Jillian a reassuring nod before he grabbed his travel pack and slipped down the gangplank, melting into the busy, twilight-lit streets of Cordovar.

As he walked, the city's sights, sounds, and scents filled his senses; the chatter of vendors, the smell of roasting chestnuts, and the hum of Cordovar's evening life. Somewhere in this maze of stone and shadow was Matax, a man with knowledge of histories most dared not touch.

The marketplace of Cordovar was alive with noise and motion as Aidan made his way through winding alleys and bustling stalls, past merchants hawking spices, textiles, and arcane relics from distant lands. The city was a sprawling hub of trade and diplomacy, a crossroads where powerful interests converged, their motives as complex as the tapestry of wares on display. Aidan kept a keen eye on his surroundings as he headed toward the familiar shopfront of Matax's apothecary.

Matax was an eccentric figure and an invaluable contact; part historian, part informant, and a true master of potions and herbal lore. His shop, tucked away in a quieter corner of the city's trade quarter, was a trove of rare elixirs, medicinal herbs, and artefacts with origins few could trace. The shop was dimly lit, and the rich smell of incense hung heavy in the air, mingling with the scent of dried herbs and oils.

As Aidan entered, Matax looked up from behind his counter, where he was carefully measuring powdered components into glass vials. A thin, wiry man with a mane of greying hair and shrewd, dark eyes, Matax had a discerning gaze that seemed to miss nothing. His attire was a blend of practicality and flair; patched leather and a worn cloak, with an emerald pendant that hinted at some arcane past.

"Aidan, my friend," Matax greeted, setting down a jar of powdered mandrake root. "You look as if the weight of the world is upon you. Here to lighten your load?"

Aidan managed a weary smile. "Perhaps. And perhaps I'm here to learn something of the world's weight, rather than shed it."

Matax's eyebrow arched. "Ah, I know that tone. Sit, then. And tell me what weighs so heavily on your mind."

Aidan took the offered seat across from Matax, clasping his hands as he leaned forward. His voice lowered, laden with an urgency he tried to temper. "I need information, Matax. Specifically, about ancient history... and certain bloodlines."

"Ancient history?" Matax echoed, his voice dipping as his fingers began to drum on the counter top. "That's a rather broad request, Aidan. Are you looking for tales of old empires or something... more obscure?"

"More obscure," Aidan replied, leaning in conspiratorially. "I'm particularly interested in the Khestar and their descendants. I've reason to believe there are groups in the city who might share this interest. Have you heard anything - anyone asking questions about them?"

Matax's gaze narrowed, his fingers stilling as he considered Aidan's words. He glanced around the shop, ensuring no customers were close enough to eavesdrop. Satisfied, he turned back to Aidan, his tone barely more than a whisper.

"The Khestar..." Matax murmured. "Now that is a name you don't hear every day. Few even remember them. The Khestar bloodline, if the legends are true, traces back to the Age of Creation, and their origins are said to be bound with forgotten magic. It's whispered that they carried knowledge not meant for mortal minds."

Aidan nodded, encouraging Matax to continue. "So, you've heard of them, then?"

"Oh, indeed," Matax said with a nod, his eyes alight with a scholar's curiosity. "But you don't come here asking about the Khestar for casual conversation, do you?"

Aidan leaned forward, his voice low. "Has anyone else been inquiring about them? Or showing unusual interest in ancient bloodlines, lost histories... that sort of thing?"

Matax scratched his chin thoughtfully, considering the question. "Now that you mention it, there have been whispers of strangers asking questions around the city. Some, I suspect, might be linked to societies whose interest in ancient lore borders on obsession."

Aidan's ears pricked up. "Such as?"

Matax's eyes darted around again, ensuring they were alone. "The Mhargrave Outreach Society, for one. They operate under the guise of historical preservation, but I have my suspicions. They've been making quiet inquiries in the archives, especially regarding lost lineages and... shall we say, the more arcane aspects of heritage. There's also been talk of The Jade Talon, though their presence is less public. Mercenaries, mostly, but with ties to powerful backers who prefer anonymity."

Aidan furrowed his brow, listening intently. "Have you heard anything about Mhorvaeus? Or his people?"

A shadow flickered across Matax's face, and he nodded gravely. "Now there's a name that makes even seasoned men like me shudder. House Mhorvaeus has influence here in Cordovar, though they rarely make their presence known. However, I've heard whispers; rumours of men with House Mhorvaeus insignias seen around the old city. Not openly, mind you, but skulking in the shadows. If Mhorvaeus is interested in the Khestar, I wouldn't doubt he has his reasons. Dark reasons, I'd wager."

Aidan's thoughts raced. House Mhorvaeus was infamous for its alliances with clandestine groups, many of whom had links to necromancy and other forbidden arts. "And what about The Silver Crescent or The Sceptre Guilds?"

"The Silver Crescent?" Matax's eyes sparkled with a mixture of amusement and caution. "Now there's a name that's been popping up more frequently. They're a cult, of sorts, though their members see themselves as scholars of the moon's hidden mysteries. They're interested in all things celestial and arcane. I wouldn't put it past them to take an interest in the Khestar, especially if they believe there's an ancient connection between the bloodline and certain lunar phenomena."

Aidan felt his pulse quicken. "And The Sceptre Guilds?"

"Ah, the Guilds," Matax said, his voice darkening. "They're more pragmatic, typically focused on material power. But even they've been rumoured to have sent envoys to the city, apparently seeking knowledge on artefacts linked to bloodlines. It's strange; their interest in such topics is new. Makes one wonder what knowledge they're after, or who they're being paid by."

Aidan absorbed this information, his mind piecing together the implications. "So, you're saying there's been a convergence of these groups here, all seemingly interested in ancient bloodlines?"

Matax nodded, his expression grave. "It's as though a magnetic force is drawing them. But beware, Aidan. For groups like these, knowledge is power, and they do not tolerate interference lightly. If they sense you're after the same answers..."

"They'll come after me," Aidan finished, his voice resolute. "But I have no choice. The Dark Aethyr Shard compels me, and I believe understanding these bloodlines may be the key to unlocking what it wants to reveal."

Matax leaned back, studying Aidan with a look of reluctant admiration. "You walk a dangerous path, my friend. But if you're determined to press on, let me tell you one more thing." He hesitated, as if weighing the wisdom of sharing it. "A few nights ago, I overheard one of Mhorvaeus's men speaking in hushed tones. He mentioned... an 'awakening' and 'preparing for a gathering of the blooded.'"

Aidan's eyes sharpened. "The blooded?"

"Yes," Matax whispered. "If I understand correctly, they're individuals with ties to ancient bloodlines; people who carry a lineage that traces back to powerful origins. Mhorvaeus and others appear to believe these bloodlines can awaken something... something old and dangerous."

Aidan's face grew tense. "And do you believe these blooded have ties to the Khestar?"

"It's a theory," Matax conceded. "But there's more. The man mentioned a gathering outside the city walls in the ruins of an ancient temple, abandoned centuries ago. The temple was built by an order dedicated to... let's just say, ancient studies. And these bloodlines you speak of - the Khestar - they may well have origins tied to such places."

Aidan clenched his fist, feeling both apprehension and determination flood him. "And this temple - how do I find it?"

Matax gave him a solemn look. "You didn't hear it from me, but follow the old trade route north, past the City of Ash. Look for a monolith shaped like a crescent; it marks the entrance to a hidden path. But take heed, Aidan. If you go there, you won't be alone."

Aidan nodded, meeting Matax's gaze with steely resolve. "Thank you, my friend. Your counsel has been invaluable, as always."

Matax placed a firm hand on Aidan's shoulder, his eyes filled with unspoken warnings. "Watch your back, Aidan. I don't want to lose one of my best clients... or a friend. The city is restless, and forces gather that even I can't fathom. The secrets you seek come with a cost."

Aidan nodded, a faint smile crossing his lips. "I'll tread carefully. And who knows? Maybe I'll return with answers that even you haven't uncovered yet."

Matax's eyes glinted with a hint of pride. "I wouldn't expect anything less. Go, Aidan. And may whatever gods watch over fools and heroes keep an eye on you."

With that, Aidan rose from his seat and made his way back through the crowded marketplace, his mind racing with new leads.

As he disappeared into the winding streets, Matax watched him go, his eyes thoughtful and shadowed with concern. Aidan was no ordinary client; he was a man driven by purpose, a seeker of truths that even the most seasoned scholars feared to unearth.

5

Scrutiny

The return journey to the Zephyr Breeze was uneventful, but Aidan's mind was abuzz with everything he'd learned from Matax. The apothecary's words hinted at deeper layers within Cordovar's underbelly, and his mind was racing with questions as he stepped back onto the deck of the airship.

He found Ahlissa on the bridge, looking out over the bustling port below. Even from this distance, Aidan could feel the energy and tension that gripped Cordovar's docks; a labyrinth of ships, crates, and bustling merchants, all under the vigilant gaze of the Cordovar port officials.

The Zephyr Breeze was no ordinary vessel; its arrival had already drawn a fair share of attention. The Cordovar docks, controlled by a shadowy and secretive organisation known as The Trust, were heavily monitored, and officials here had little patience for unknown influences.

No sooner had Aidan set foot on deck than Jalik, one of Ahlissa's trusted officers, approached her with a look of quiet urgency.

"Commander," he reported, his voice low but steady. "We've detected significant divination magic directed at us. Cordovar's port authorities appear to be scrying the Zephyr Breeze, examining us from a distance."

Ahlissa barely reacted, her eyes fixed on the city skyline as if the intrusion were of little concern. With a small, amused smile, she replied, "Lower the primary anti-divination shields, Jalik. Let them see only what we want them to see; legal cargo and personnel. Keep the shard's compartment and the representative's quarters fully shielded. Our guests and restricted items must remain beyond their gaze. Inform the crew to be vigilant, especially near sensitive areas, and keep all visual illusions in place to deter any physical inspection."

"Yes, Commander." Jalik offered a crisp nod and strode off, relaying her instructions to the rest of the crew.

Ahlissa turned to Aidan, her expression softened by a hint of mirth. "As you can see, the people of Cordovar are rather paranoid about maintaining their peace. The Trust has eyes everywhere and considers any outsider a potential threat. They've known of my past associations and, as expected, are deeply curious about my present ones. While they think they know me, they know only what I permit them to know, and that unsettles them."

Aidan nodded, listening carefully. "So, you give them just enough to satisfy their curiosity, but keep the real matters hidden?"

"Precisely," she replied, folding her arms. "We don't want to alarm them, but we also don't reveal everything. My associations with groups like the Kale Khestari and the ancient families arouse suspicion, but I keep the true extent of my work carefully veiled. We won't be here long;

only enough time for me to complete some private business. You're free to go ashore again, if you wish. There's a library here you might find intriguing, given your scholarly interests. It takes up nearly a quarter of the city, and it is filled with knowledge spanning centuries."

Aidan's eyes lit up, and he couldn't hide his curiosity. "The library here is that large? I didn't know."

Ahlissa chuckled, her eyes gleaming with a mix of amusement and pride. "Yes, it's one of the oldest and most comprehensive libraries in this part of the world. Cordovar may be insular, but they take great pride in their collection of knowledge. You should take advantage of it, while you're here. But remember, we depart at dusk."

Aidan's gaze drifted over the skyline, taking in the city's sprawling architecture as he considered her suggestion. "Thank you, Ahlissa. I think I'll head there now. I'll see if Jillian wants to join me. But there's also something else I've learnt from my visit with Matax that I think you should know."

Ahlissa raised an eyebrow with curiosity "So, Matax gave you another breadcrumb to follow? This hidden temple; do you think it's worth pursuing?"

Aidan nodded "He mentioned a crescent-shaped monolith marking the path. It's along an old trade route north of Cordovar, past somewhere called the City of Ash. Supposedly, Mhorvaeus' people have been whispering about preparations there for a gathering of something they call 'The Blooded.'"

"'The Blooded'? Sounds like a cult. And cults usually spell trouble."

Ahlissa replied.

"Exactly. He wasn't sure of the details, but it's suspicious enough to warrant keeping an eye on. If Mhorvaeus is involved, it's bound to connect to the larger picture. Maybe even to the shard." Aidan agreed.

Ahlissa spoke thoughtfully "Agreed, but let's not divert focus just yet. The shard is our priority. Once we've unlocked more of its secrets and understand where it's leading us, we'll circle back to this temple."

Aidan nodded "Noted. I'll mark it for future investigation. If it is a cult, we'll need to tread carefully. Especially if they're gathering in force. Knowing Mhorvaeus' established connections, it's most likely to be something to do with The Servants of Aroth."

"Careful's not always our style, but point taken. We'll keep it on the list – for after we know more." Ahlissa said, with a wry smile.

"Understood. One thing at a time," Aidan replied.

He made his way below deck to where Jillian's quarters were, his footsteps echoing softly in the ship's corridors. Pausing outside her door, he knocked politely, hearing a soft shuffle before the door creaked open. Jillian appeared, her face brightening with a gentle smile when she saw him.

"Oh, hello, Aidan. You look ready for an adventure," she greeted, noting the eager look in his eyes.

Aidan returned her smile. "I'm heading to the library. Apparently, it's massive; spans a good quarter of the city. I thought you might want to come along?"

Jillian's smile faltered, a thoughtful shadow crossing her features. "That's a kind offer, Aidan, but I think I'll stay aboard the ship this time. The Cordovar authorities... they scrutinize everyone, especially outsiders. Given my lineage, I think it's wiser for me to keep a low profile. Even though I could conceal myself with illusions, it's better if they see me as just another crew member."

Aidan nodded, understanding her caution. "I hadn't considered that, but it makes sense. I'll keep a low profile myself."

She reached out, giving his arm a brief, reassuring squeeze. "Be careful, Aidan. Cordovar is a beautiful place, but it's full of secrets. Watch your step."

With a grateful nod, Aidan turned back up the steps, adjusting the worn leather strap of his travel pack. He dressed in robes, a simple garb for scholars that he hoped would deflect attention. As he strode down the gangplank, he heard Ahlissa call out behind him.

"I'll see you in a few hours, Aidan. Dusk, remember, so don't be late," she reminded him. "We are also expecting to receive the team of experts that Mistress Sainar promised, from the New Kanarzand Bureau of Forbidden Archaeology this evening."

Aidan nodded, gave a wave over his shoulder, then made his way into the heart of Cordovar.

6

Streetwise

After leaving the port, Aidan found himself engulfed by Cordovar's bustling streets. The city seemed like an endless maze of narrow alleys, winding passageways, and cobblestone streets lined with multi storied buildings that loomed overhead, casting elongated shadows under the sun. The architecture was a blend of old-world charm and practicality, with buildings adorned with balconies that spilled over with bright, exotic flowers and windows decorated in stained glass.

One of the first things Aidan noticed was the extraordinary diversity of people filling the streets. The city was a mosaic of cultures, its residents an eclectic mix from across the continent. Young Adeni scholars, recognizable by their simple yet elegant robes, were in the majority; their lively conversations and laughter filled the air as they navigated the crowded streets, books clutched in their arms. Interspersed among them were Argar and Aystar individuals, many of whom wore attire that distinguished their respective cultural identities. Aidan observed that, unlike the bustling ports he'd grown used to, Cordovar's residents seemed genuinely at ease here, the city's energy vibrant but harmonious.

As he moved through the crowds, his attention was drawn to a small group of Argar in dark robes embroidered with silver thread, their symbols marking them as members of the So-Kech; the "Word Bearers." This order held a special place in Argar society, respected as guardians of ancient knowledge and secrets from the days of the Argar Empire. Aidan observed their dignified mannerisms and reverent demeanour, recognizing the deep sense of purpose that accompanied them.

The sight stirred memories within him, transporting him back to an incident in Gideon City when he was a trainee scholar - a city infamous for its strict regulations and xenophobic attitudes. He recalled the tense night he'd spent in Gideon's grand museum and library complex, where he'd crossed paths with one of these So-Kech followers. The sorcerer had been trying to steal an artefact of ancient importance, a relic he claimed belonged to the Argar people. The encounter had nearly sparked a diplomatic incident, as the Gideon authorities had vehemently objected to the So-Kech's presence, seeing their outpost as a threat to the city's carefully guarded neutrality. It was a stark contrast to the peaceful, if bustling, streets of Cordovar.

Aidan's path wound through several quadrangles, small open squares nestled between buildings where vibrant street performances took place. Musicians played instruments that produced strange, haunting melodies; dancers spun in colourful robes; jugglers tossed flaming torches high into the air. These small performances seemed to embody the city's spirit, as onlookers gathered in circles, clapping, laughing, and cheering the performers on. Aidan was struck by the light-heartedness of it all. There was no tension, no underlying malice, just a city alive with the joy of shared moments. It was a rare thing to witness in his line of work, where danger and secrets often clouded his view of the world.

Continuing onward, Aidan passed rows of small, family-owned shops, each specializing in a unique trade. There were jewellers displaying glittering gemstones, alchemists grinding herbs in brass mortars, herbalists arranging dried bundles of rare plants, mapmakers carefully inking the contours of distant lands, and antiquarians handling artefacts with a reverence usually reserved for relics of faith. The air was thick with a blend of scents; herbs, spices, incense, and the occasional whiff of something metallic or smoky wafting from the forge of an artificer's workshop.

The city's calm buzz was refreshing, yet Aidan felt a prickling awareness that something was amiss. As he turned down a particularly narrow street, he sensed a subtle shift in the atmosphere. He hadn't noticed at first, but a feeling had crept up on him - a sense of being watched. He cast a discreet glance over his shoulder and caught sight of a figure moving through the shadows, keeping pace with him while staying just out of direct view. The figure lingered in the alleys, sliding between the shadows of overhanging balconies and darting out of sight whenever Aidan turned his head.

Aidan's heart beat faster, but he kept his pace steady, feigning nonchalance. He'd learned long ago that the best way to deal with a tail was to act unaware; sudden changes in pace or direction would only confirm their suspicions. Instead, he let his mind work over the possibilities.

Was this one of Mhorvaeus's spies? The thought was unsettling but plausible; Cordovar was a prime hub for information, and House Mhorvaeus was known to have extensive networks. Ahlissa had warned him that their presence would likely be noted, so perhaps his follower was a routine observer, a spy simply doing his job.

He continued to walk, keeping his senses heightened, but he was increasingly aware of another, more invasive presence; a feeling that someone was watching him, but not from the shadows. This sensation was far more subtle, an intangible prickling on his skin that seemed to follow him since he'd left the Zephyr Breeze.

It was the unmistakable effect of divination magic; a scrying spell, perhaps. Aidan's mind raced. The Trust's port authorities were thorough, and their spies undoubtedly skilled, but this felt different. This was someone's attempt to follow his every move, even though they remained hidden from sight.

He focused on maintaining a casual, steady demeanour as he processed the situation. Whoever was tracking him wanted more than just a quick glance; they sought detailed knowledge of his movements, his interactions. Aidan tightened his mental defences, grounding his thoughts in the here and now, hoping to limit what the scrying spell could glean from him. He was no stranger to countering such magic, though it was difficult to block entirely without preparation.

The cobbled streets soon led him to a series of ornate signs pointing toward Cordovar's grand library. Relieved to have a clear destination, he followed the signs, glancing at shop windows as he passed, using their reflections to keep tabs on the figure trailing him. The shadow moved deftly through the crowd, sticking to darkened alcoves and alleys, slipping away whenever Aidan got too close to catching a glimpse.

He made his way down another narrow street lined with rows of flowering vines hanging from wrought iron railings, the scent of jasmine thick in the air. The sounds of the street performers faded as he approached a quieter area. The buildings here had an aged elegance, with weathered facades that hinted at centuries of history. At last, he caught sight of the library's entrance; a grand archway flanked by massive stone statues of mythic beasts, each one holding a torch that seemed to burn with a perpetual flame.

Standing before the entrance, he felt a small surge of relief, though he knew he was far from free of scrutiny. He cast another glance behind him, noticing his shadowy follower keeping a careful distance, clearly intent on blending in with the evening's foot traffic. Aidan was tempted to confront the figure directly, but he decided against it. For now, he had no clear understanding of who they served or why they tracked him. Confrontation would likely draw more attention than he could afford in a city already teeming with watchful eyes.

Instead, he straightened his robe, adjusting his hood to shade his face as he ascended the stone steps toward the library. As he moved, the sense of divination magic lingered like a thin, invisible thread connecting him to some unseen watcher. Whoever they were, they were skilled enough to mask their origin. He resisted the urge to look for the source, reminding himself that his focus was the library and the knowledge it held.

Before entering the towering doors of the library, he stole a final glance at the crowd. The figure that had been following him was nowhere in sight; perhaps they had melted back into the labyrinthine alleys, content to wait for his return. The scrying presence, however, remained, hovering like an unseen observer peering through a veil.

Steeling himself, Aidan took a deep breath and pushed open the heavy doors of the library.

7

The Library

Aidan stood before the entrance to the grand Cordovar Library, a towering structure hewn from ancient stone and adorned with intricate carvings depicting mythic scenes from the city's deep history. The massive double doors, easily forty feet high and bound in reinforced metalwork, swung inward soundlessly as he approached, revealing a vaulted hall lined with reading desks and lit by an ethereal glow that seemed to emanate from the very walls. A soft hum filled the air, as if centuries of whispered knowledge had taken root here, creating an atmosphere that was both calming and humbling.

Stepping into the library's main hall, Aidan took a moment to orient himself, his gaze sweeping over the vast chamber. Rows of desks filled the space, some occupied by scholars bent over thick tomes or whispering animatedly among themselves. To his left, he noticed a modest sign mounted above an arched doorway that directed new visitors to a processing room.

Following the sign, Aidan entered a smaller room lined with book-shelves containing neatly folded pamphlets. Above a small stand was a sign reading "Take One." Curious, Aidan picked up a brochure and leafed through it. The pamphlet provided a brief summary of the library's history, explaining its centuries-old dedication to preserving knowledge from across Scylla and beyond. The Cordovar Library, he read, had withstood countless wars, internal disputes, and even periods of censorship, emerging each time as a stronger repository of the world's wisdom.

While Aidan absorbed the pamphlet's contents, an eager young usher bustled over from behind a large wooden counter, where a scribe was taking notes. The usher was a small, animated scholar, practically radiating excitement as he approached.

"Hello! You must be new here," the young usher exclaimed, his eyes alight with curiosity. "I love your robe! It matches your eyes splendidly. What brings you to the library today?"

Caught slightly off guard, Aidan managed a polite smile. "I'm just visiting the city and thought I should explore the library. I've heard wonderful things about it."

"Ah, very wise indeed," the usher responded, nodding sagely. "The library is a treasure beyond compare! And what is it that interests you? What subject speaks to you most? Mathematics? Astronomy? History?"

"Yes... history," Aidan replied, sensing that a simple answer would keep things moving.

The young scholar made a face, his excitement momentarily replaced by disappointment. "History? Oh, I find it terribly dull, myself. All those dates and names. Mathematics, now that's useful! Practical, especially when it comes to money. But history..." He sighed, shaking his head in a way that made Aidan suppress a smile.

"Indeed. Mathematics has its charms," Aidan agreed diplomatically.

"Right then!" the usher declared, snapping back to attention. "Follow me, and I'll assign you to a guide from the university. He'll show you to the sections that suit your... interests."

The usher led Aidan deeper into the processing area, where he was introduced to a rather colourful individual named Gladstone. Dressed in an eye-catching combination of bright yellows, oranges, and greens, all topped by a voluminous red cloak, Gladstone cut an unusual figure. He was middle-aged, though still considered a young scholar by Cordovar standards, and his wild, optimistic demeanour was tempered by a slight limp and a nervous twitch in his right hand.

Gladstone extended a hand enthusiastically. "Very pleased to meet you, sir! And may I ask, where are you from? You have an air of the traveller about you."

"Gideon," Aidan replied, clasping the man's hand in a firm handshake.

"Gideon! Oh, how marvellous!" Gladstone exclaimed, his eyes widening with genuine excitement. "We don't often get scholars from Gideon here. Research grants from your institutions, I'm afraid, have been dwindling, especially since The Thirteen tightened their grip on what can be studied."

Aidan frowned slightly. "I didn't realise restrictions had gotten that severe."

"Oh, it's quite the topic of conversation among scholars here," Gladstone went on. "Any request from Gideon to study history, or any subjects remotely connected to certain... ancient paths, are often rejected outright. It's rather curious, don't you think? Why would such learned individuals restrict knowledge in a city like Gideon, known for its libraries and educational prowess?"

Aidan nodded, a hint of concern crossing his face. "Very curious indeed. I trained under Master Brevax, who managed the library at Kanarzand before moving to Gideon."

Gladstone's eyes lit up at the mention of Brevax. "Master Brevax! A legend, that one. A scholar of the highest order! So you're one of his students?"

"I worked with him for years," Aidan replied. "Before... well, before the Darkness."

Gladstone's expression softened, and he gave a solemn nod. "The Darkness... yes, a tragic chapter for Kanarzand. They say it was foretold in prophecy, but some claim it was also punishment for the mages' transgressions. We heard they were hostile toward non-Adeni races and outsiders. I'd be fascinated to hear what happened from someone who lived it. Tell me, what role did you play in those dark times?"

Aidan hesitated, his gaze drifting briefly as memories flooded back. "Let's just say, my part is... complicated. One day, I'll document the details. It's a story that may surprise you."

"Oh, I look forward to that day!" Gladstone said with an excited grin. "Now, then; to business! Are there any particular subjects or items you seek here? Or will we be browsing general collections today?"

"Mostly general research. I came to admire the library, but if I find resources worth studying, I'll plan a return visit. For now, I have only a few hours."

"Understood!" Gladstone exclaimed. "Let's proceed to the catalogues."

The guide led Aidan down a series of hallways, through doors that opened in intricate geometric patterns before silently reassembling once they'd passed. They reached an antique metal elevator, which carried them down nearly a hundred feet. At the bottom, they emerged onto a narrow landing that led through winding corridors and down a spiral metal staircase until they finally arrived at a stone doorway, scarcely five feet high. Gladstone, undeterred by the cramped quarters, opened the door to reveal an enormous, dimly lit room lined with towering catalogue cabinets that reached up sixty feet.

"This, my friend," Gladstone announced with a flourish, "is the Catalogue Room! Every record, every scroll, every tome in the library is documented here. You can locate whatever your heart desires, though it may take some patience. I'm here to assist with expediency, of course."

He led Aidan to a massive wooden ladder mounted on rails, which glided along the aisles. They climbed to a platform about forty feet up, where Gladstone scanned the shelves until he found a drawer marked in early Aystaran script, an archaic dialect Aidan recognised from his studies. The drawer contained numerous manuscripts detailing the accepted history of the Kale Khestari, recounting their rise after the Age of Creation. The histories spoke of how they conquered lands in Southeast Scylla, waging brutal campaigns against the disorganised

Argar tribes that lived there.

Aidan sifted through the documents, searching for any mention of progenitors or ancient figures that might hint at forgotten origins. "Interesting," he muttered, pausing at a reference to a location known as the Star Haunt. The Kale Khestari, the document claimed, had kept a respectful distance from the place, which they believed was haunted by malevolent spirits from an era predating their own.

"A curious detail," Aidan remarked, making a mental note.

Gladstone leaned over, clearly fascinated. "Yes, the Star Haunt has always been a place of mystery. The Kale Khestari would not dare approach it, nor have most historians succeeded in explaining its significance. It appears you may have uncovered a thread worth pulling on, my friend."

One name caught Aidan's eye; *The Schism*, authored by someone named Athovhar. The text appeared to explore the growing tensions between the Kale Khestari and the elves of Kharadia, stemming from the Khestari's decision to abandon traditional reverence for the deathless in favour of ancestor worship.

"Athovhar," Aidan murmured, the name familiar. It was the same name as the revered representative aboard the Zephyr Breeze.

"If I were to request a copy of this particular book," Aidan inquired, "how much would it cost me?"

Gladstone pursed his lips thoughtfully. "A rare volume, indeed. Such requests are free, but given its rarity, copying could take a month, and the cost may run around 1,000 gold sovereigns. We offer payment plans if that helps soften the blow, or we accept items of scholarly value."

"I see," Aidan replied. "Perhaps my writings on the fall of Kanarzand might be of interest. My experiences there could contribute to the library's records."

Gladstone's face lit up. "Oh, yes! First-hand accounts are invaluable. I'd be delighted to introduce your work to our collections. If you bring us samples next time, we'd happily consider them."

Aidan reached into his pack and withdrew a small book, bound in indigo leather, known simply as *The Blue*. It contained his observations from his time in Kanarzand, along with notes on the Darkness and the ruins left behind.

"This is intriguing," Gladstone said, thumbing through the book. "A first-hand account like this is indeed rare and would be highly prized by our archives. I'll make the request for *The Schism* and ensure a scribe is assigned to copy it when you return. Now, do you have other subjects of interest?"

Aidan shook his head, noting the time. "I'd like to return better prepared, with a clearer idea of what I need. But what I've seen today is remarkable."

Puffing up with pride, Gladstone handed him a card with his name engraved in elaborate script. "Ask for me personally when you next return."

Aidan accepted the card with a nod. "Thank you, Gladstone. I'll be sure to do that."

Gladstone guided him back to the library's entrance, making small talk along the way. As they reached the foyer, Aidan thanked him once more before stepping outside into the afternoon sun.

He hadn't gone more than a few paces when a young man, dressed in garish hues of red and purple and sporting a wide-brimmed hat, darted out of the crowd and blocked his path with an eager grin.

"Good day to you, Aidan!" the man greeted, thrusting out a hand. "They call me Wrangler, a reporter for the *Cordovar Chronicle*! Would you spare a moment to answer a few questions?"

Aidan hesitated, trying to sidestep him. "I'm not here for interviews."

"Oh, come now," Wrangler persisted, undeterred. "What brings you to Cordovar? Business? Adventure? Research? Did you uncover anything noteworthy in the library? Perhaps an exclusive artefact?"

Aidan sighed. "I'm here for research. Nothing more."

Wrangler's eyes twinkled with excitement, ignoring Aidan's attempts to brush him off. "Are you hiding something, perhaps? Did you witness the fall of Kanarzand? What was it like? Were you scared? Some even say you faced down Izen'draazt! A hero, no?"

"How do you know my name?" Aidan asked, suspicion lacing his tone.

Wrangler chuckled, tapping the side of his nose. "We're the *Chronicle*, sir. We know everyone, and we never miss a good story! Why, we even have eyewitness accounts of you dancing with Lady Ahlissa at the Liberty Spire! Are you two... an item? Or just a fleeting romance?"

Aidan raised an eyebrow, mildly annoyed. "I assure you, Lady Ahlissa and I are not romantically involved."

Wrangler grinned, undeterred. "Oh? So no scandal there, then? Perhaps we could pay for a touch of heartbreak in the story; tears sell, you know!"

Aidan shot him a wry smile. "Sorry to disappoint, but I'm genuinely happy for her."

Wrangler looked momentarily deflated, but quickly rebounded. "Well, exclusive news nonetheless! Aidan from Gideon vows to publish his memoirs on the fall of Kanarzand!" Wrangler said excitedly, his quill poised above a notepad. "Would you be open to offering excerpts to the *Chronicle*?"

"Perhaps," Aidan allowed, giving a nod of polite dismissal before slipping back into the bustling crowd. He could still hear Wrangler shouting behind him, "We'll be in touch for that interview when your book's out, Aidan! Don't forget!"

Shaking his head, Aidan quickened his pace toward the docks, eager to return to the relative sanctuary of the Zephyr Breeze. His brief experience in the library had opened new questions - and stirred more attention - than he'd anticipated, but he knew he'd be back. Cordovar, for all its quirks and relentless reporters, was proving to be an unexpected treasure trove.

8

Dark Agents

After leaving the library, Aidan retraced his steps through Cordovar's winding streets, eager to return to the Zephyr Breeze and sift through the knowledge he'd uncovered. But as he reached the main thoroughfare, he found his original path blocked by an elaborate procession of street entertainers. Jugglers, dancers, musicians, and acrobats paraded in colourful costumes, filling the street with sound and movement. The crowd had gathered thickly, watching the spectacle with rapt attention, making it nearly impossible for Aidan to pass.

He sighed and looked around, hoping to find an alternate route. Nearby, a group of small Argar loitered near a jeweller's stall, chatting in their native tongue. Aidan approached them, raising his voice above the crowd's noise. "Excuse me, friends. I need to find my way back to the airship docks. Could you direct me?"

One of the Argar, a young one with a crooked smile, squinted up at Aidan and then nodded. "Ahh, that way," he said, gesturing down a narrow street that diverged from the main road.

"Thank you," Aidan replied, setting off in the direction the goblin had indicated. He moved through the unfamiliar streets, weaving past family-owned shops, workshops, and market stalls that sold everything from rare herbs to mechanical trinkets. He noted the tall buildings crowding the alleyways, each story leaning over the narrow streets, casting long shadows that deepened as evening crept over the city.

As he ventured deeper into the maze of alleyways, he realised the air was growing quieter, the noise from the main streets receding until he could hear only the muffled sounds of distant footfalls and occasional voices drifting from open windows. Aidan pressed on, following the unfamiliar streets with a sense of vague unease.

Suddenly, just as he was about to turn a corner, the wall of a nearby building seemed to shimmer and dissolve, revealing a hidden alcove. Before he could react, two large, muscular figures lunged at him from the shadows, seizing his arms in iron grips.

"Be quiet," a gruff voice commanded, its tone dripping with menace. "Don't struggle."

Aidan barely had time to open his mouth before a thick, rough-spun hood was pulled over his head, blocking out the light. His captors dragged him forward, their grips unyielding as they steered him through a series of turns. He stumbled once, and they hauled him back to his feet with rough impatience. He tried to get his bearings, counting steps, listening to the muffled sounds of their footfalls, but the path they took twisted unpredictably, leaving him disoriented.

At last, they came to a halt. Aidan heard a door creak open, then felt himself pushed forward and forced down onto a hard wooden chair.

The ropes they used to bind him bit into his wrists and ankles, making escape impossible. A moment later, the hood was yanked off, and Aidan blinked against the sudden dim light.

He found himself in a small, dank wine cellar. The walls were lined with old casks, and the air was thick with the sour smell of ageing wood and mildew. Two masked men stood before him, their faces obscured by black leather masks that left only their eyes visible. Their attire was plain, but Aidan noted the subtle yet distinct accents in their voices. He listened carefully, recognizing hints of Sindarri inflection, a rough accent from the northern lands. A connection to Sindarr meant they could be working for Mhorvaeus; something he'd feared might happen from the moment he'd set foot in Cordovar.

One of the men stepped forward, crossing his arms as he examined Aidan with a cold, calculating gaze. "We're going to have a little chat," he said in a slow, mocking drawl. "Let's start simple. Why have you come to Cordovar?"

Aidan kept his expression neutral. "To visit the university," he replied evenly.

The man raised an eyebrow, though Aidan could only guess his expression beneath the mask. "Oh, really? And what were you hoping to find in the library?"

"I wanted to see what the library contained," Aidan replied smoothly. "It was simply research for a potential book."

The second man, a shorter, stockier figure, let out a snort of disbelief. "Research? And what topic might that be?"

"History," Aidan replied. "Particularly, the history of Gideon."

The man cocked his head, clearly unimpressed. "And who, exactly, do you work for?"

"My research is my own," Aidan answered calmly. "I'm a crew member of the Zephyr Breeze."

The taller man, evidently growing impatient, retrieved a long, sharp knife from the wall and began pacing. He was silent for a moment, letting the blade glint ominously in the low light. Finally, he looked back at Aidan. "I'll ask you again: who do you work for?"

Aidan met his gaze with steely resolve. "As I said, I work for myself. I'm just a scholar and a crew member. Ahlissa often needs my translation skills; that's all."

The man let out a low, disdainful chuckle. "Don't insult my intelligence. We both know you do more than that. What business are you conducting for her?"

Aidan held his ground, keeping his voice even. "I'm conducting no business for her. My visit to the library was my own. I'm gathering material to write a book."

The shorter man shook his head in annoyance, while the tall man flexed his hands, cracking his knuckles one by one. "Tell me more about this 'book' you intend to write," he demanded.

"It's about my experiences in Kanarzand," Aidan replied, noting the flicker of curiosity in the man's eyes.

The taller man's voice dropped to a sceptical growl. "And who, exactly, do you think would want to read that?"

"Many people," Aidan replied coolly. "The university, for one. I was one of the few to witness what happened in Kanarzand. Historians value first-hand accounts."

The man leaned in closer, his voice dripping with suspicion. "And what, exactly, did you see in Kanarzand?"

"I saw the arrival of Izen'draazt," Aidan replied, his voice a mixture of bitterness and defiance.

The tall man's expression hardened, his eyes narrowing behind the mask. "What was your job in Kanarzand?"

"I worked at the library," Aidan said simply, watching their reactions carefully.

The second man glanced at his partner, then back at Aidan. "So you'd be familiar with its former patron, Lord Khannay?"

"Yes," Aidan said, knowing he was treading dangerous ground. "I knew who he was, if that's what you're asking."

The tall man leaned forward, his voice deadly quiet. "Tell us what you think he was."

Aidan let a faint smile touch his lips. "He was a vampire."

The man's grip tightened on his knife, and he leaned even closer. "How did you find that out?"

"I researched it," Aidan replied, sensing the man's growing frustration. "You'd be surprised what one can learn in a library."

The shorter man muttered something under his breath, and the tall man's face twisted in anger. Without warning, he lashed out, striking Aidan across the face with a brutal backhand. Pain shot through Aidan's cheek, and he tasted blood in his mouth.

"Don't get smart with us," the tall man growled. "Let's get back to your work on the Zephyr Breeze. As a crew member, do they pay you well?"

Aidan spat blood to the side, his tone unyielding. "Money doesn't interest me much. I work with good people; the crew and Ahlissa."

The tall man's eyes narrowed, and without a word, he struck Aidan again, harder this time. "If money doesn't interest you, then what does? You think you're above loyalty?"

"If you're trying to buy me, don't bother. I'm not interested," Aidan said, his voice steady despite the pain.

The man hit him again, then held the knife close to Aidan's throat, the sharp edge pressing against his skin. "You're testing my patience. Tell me what's on board the Zephyr Breeze. We know there's something valuable hidden there. Describe it."

Aidan held his ground, staring defiantly back at his captor. "Yes, there's cargo on board. But as for what's hidden, your employer should know better than to pry into other people's business."

The short man made a sound of irritation, but the tall man's face contorted with fury. He leaned in, pressing the knife closer. "We know you took something from beneath Gideon City - an artefact. Describe it."

Aidan gave a faint shrug, wincing against the blade's pressure. "We found a box in the ruins, yes. It was being excavated by a vampire, who didn't survive the encounter. We took the box, but I wasn't there when it was opened. I believe it's an Aystaran artefact, but it's dangerous. Your master won't be able to touch it without being harmed."

The tall man's face contorted with rage. He struck Aidan once more, then paused, raising the knife to Aidan's throat again. "What do you know about the demise of Baron Von-Claagen beneath Gideon City?"

Aidan smiled faintly through the pain. "We destroyed him. Fire bolts, actually. Very effective."

The man's grip faltered, and he stepped back, clearly startled. "So it was you," he muttered. "Our Master is deeply displeased with what happened. You will return what you took."

He raised the knife, and his partner murmured something, looking anxious. But before he could strike again, the short man held up his hand. "Wait."

The short man reached into his cloak and pulled out a small, smooth obsidian stone. He held it in his palm, and a faint, wavering light began to emit from its surface. An image materialized; a shadowy figure Aidan recognised at once as Mhorvaeus, his face obscured in shadow, his voice a slow, menacing hiss.

"What have you learned?" Mhorvaeus inquired, his voice echoing in the silence.

The tall man straightened, bowing slightly. "Master, he tells us nothing. He resists."

Mhorvaeus tilted his head, his expression almost amused. "So, there is defiance in this one. Interesting. Let him go."

The tall man's shoulders tensed in surprise. "Master, won't he alert the authorities? The Trust will be alerted -"

Mhorvaeus dismissed the concern with a flick of his hand. "The Trust cannot detect you. I've seen to that. Release him."

Both men bowed respectfully, and the image faded, leaving them in silence. The tall man turned to Aidan, his expression grudgingly respectful. "You heard the Master. Consider yourself lucky."

Aidan's sense of relief was short-lived as the tall man drew back his fist one final time, landing a heavy blow that left Aidan's vision swimming. His consciousness slipped, and he felt himself slump forward, darkness claiming him.

When Aidan came to, he was lying in an alleyway, his head throbbing, his face sore from the repeated blows. The faint sound of footsteps reached his ears, and he squinted up to see two city constables standing over him, their expressions a mixture of concern and suspicion.

"What happened to you?" one of them asked, offering a hand to help him sit up.

Aidan accepted the help, wincing. "I was... ambushed. A couple of men dragged me off. I was roughed up, but they didn't take anything."

The constable exchanged a glance with his partner. "Where are you from?"

"I'm with the Zephyr Breeze," Aidan replied, still trying to shake off the lingering haze. "I'd just come from the library."

The constable raised an eyebrow, clearly impressed. "Ah, so you travel with Lady Ahlissa's crew. Quite the reputation her ship has."

"As does your university," Aidan said, managing a faint, wry smile.

The constable looked pleased at the compliment. "Very well, then. What's your name?"

"Aidan," he replied, straightening.

The constable nodded approvingly. "Well, Aidan, you should report this attack if you want to pursue it. Stop by the station near the air docks. We don't see much crime in Cordovar, but we'll be on the lookout. Any descriptions of your attackers?"

"Both were hooded. One tall, one short. They took me to a wine cellar, but I don't know where," Aidan said.

"Not much to go on, but file a report if you wish," the constable advised. "Now get those injuries looked at. They're minor, but better safe than sorry."

Aidan nodded in thanks, accepting their directions back to the air docks. As he limped away, he couldn't shake Mhorvaeus's final words. Watch your back. Do not trust those you think you know.

With every step toward the Zephyr Breeze, Aidan felt the weight of those words pressing down, knowing that his journey had just grown infinitely more perilous.

9

Return to the Zephyr Breeze

Aidan staggered up the gangplank of the Zephyr Breeze, his face bruised, and his gait unsteady from the beating he'd endured at the hands of Mhorvaeus's agents. The familiar sight of the ship brought him a small measure of relief, but he couldn't ignore the simmering anger that gnawed at him. His mind replayed every detail of the interrogation; the sharp words, the mocking questions, and Mhorvaeus's hissing voice in that cold, dead language.

As he reached the main deck, Ahlissa and Jillian appeared from the ship's inner quarters, their faces taut with concern the moment they saw him.

"Aidan!" Ahlissa exclaimed, her eyes widening as she took in his battered appearance. "What happened? You look terrible. Did someone _"

"Two of Mhorvaeus's henchmen," Aidan interrupted, his voice rough and tired. "They ambushed me in an alleyway on my way back. Hooded me, dragged me off to a cellar. I was in there with them for what felt like hours."

Ahlissa's expression darkened. "What... here, in Cordovar? One of the most protected cities, and devoted to peace, in all of Scylla?"

"Yes," Aidan replied grimly, his mouth twisting in a bitter smile. "Even here. They wanted information about what we're carrying on board."

Jillian's gaze sharpened, worry deepening in her eyes. "And what did you tell them?"

Aidan met her gaze steadily. "Nothing specific. I mentioned that it's an Aystaran artefact and that's all. They seemed frustrated, but then..." He paused, swallowing against the bitterness in his throat. "Then I saw an image of Mhorvaeus. He spoke in that same chilling language we heard the last time we encountered him, but it was the henchmen who mentioned something... a group called the Trust."

Ahlissa's face lightened with recognition. "Yes... the Trust is Cordovar's secret police force. I warned you about them before our arrival. They're everywhere, always vigilant, guarding the city's peace through any means necessary. Did Mhorvaeus speak of them directly?"

"No, it was his agent who brought them up," Aidan replied. "But Mhorvaeus didn't seem concerned about their presence. It was almost as though he had measures in place to keep them oblivious to his activities. His men also let slip something else; the Baron Von-Claagen that we encountered beneath Gideon? He was one of Mhorvaeus's servants. That whole expedition... it was Mhorvaeus's."

Jillian drew in a sharp breath. "Then they know we have the artefact. It wasn't random; they've been watching us."

Ahlissa's eyes flashed with indignation. "It's disturbing that Mhorvaeus has spies who could follow us even here, and that they knew about the shielded area on the ship. We'll need to heighten our defences."

"Agreed," Aidan said, rubbing his sore wrist absently. "The more questions they asked, the more I learned about what they know. They were furious about the Baron's death. I told them it was a team effort, but I admitted that I was the one who identified him as a vampire. They mentioned Lord Khannay, too."

Ahlissa pressed her lips into a thin line. "Mhorvaeus has every reason to be furious that the Baron is dead. It seems he's far more involved in the affairs of Gideon than we'd anticipated."

"They didn't let their frustration stop them from dealing out some 'discipline'," Aidan said with a wry smile, gesturing to the bruises on his face and arms. "They weren't exactly gentle."

Ahlissa's expression softened, though her eyes still held an edge of determination. "You need to rest and regain your strength. I've prepared for you to interact with the shard alone, but only once you've recovered fully. I don't want you approaching it in a weakened state; it can be... unpredictable."

Aidan nodded, grateful for her concern. "I agree and thank you. Oh, by the way, the library visit was productive. I found references to artefacts similar to the one we retrieved, and a book written by Athovhar. It might be significant."

Ahlissa's eyebrows lifted slightly. "That's promising news. Tell me all about it after you've rested. I'll ensure you're undisturbed until you've fully recovered."

Jillian moved to Aidan's side, gently placing a hand on his shoulder. "Come on, let's get you to your room. I'll bring some healing and sleeping potions to help with your recovery."

She led him below deck to his quarters, where he eased himself onto the small cot, sighing as he leaned back against the soft bedding. Jillian handed him two small vials, one filled with a pale blue liquid and the other with a warm amber glow.

"Drink these," she urged softly, watching him with a concerned gaze. "You need proper rest, Aidan. I feared the worst when you didn't return on time. Seeing you injured like this..."

He took the vials from her and downed the blue one first, its cool, refreshing effect spreading through his sore muscles and bruised skin. Then he drank the amber potion, feeling warmth pool in his stomach, slowly drifting into his veins like liquid sunlight.

"I'll be alright after some rest," he assured her, trying to muster a reassuring smile. "They roughed me up, but it was nothing too serious."

Jillian gave a small nod, though her worry remained. "Rest well, Aidan. I'm glad you made it back without greater harm. Things have been quiet here, though I kept expecting trouble after you didn't return. There's been no activity with the shard."

Aidan murmured his thanks, his eyelids growing heavy as the potions began to work. He heard her footsteps fade down the hallway, leaving him alone in the soft stillness of his cabin. The gentle sway of the ship as it lifted from the port and drifted toward the open skies provided a soothing rhythm, lulling him into a deep, dreamless sleep.

10

Alone with the Shard

The Zephyr Breeze glided smoothly over the northern skies, Cordovar now a distant blur as it sailed toward open land. Ahlissa had confirmed there were no signs of pursuit, yet the weight of recent events seemed to press heavily on the ship and its crew. Over breakfast, Ahlissa, Aidan, and Jillian gathered on a private deck attached to the rear of the command bridge, their view open to the cloud-streaked skies behind them.

As they settled into their meal, Ahlissa turned to Aidan, her expression calm but serious. "Aidan, you're free to study the shard as you see fit," she said, her tone direct. "Just you, though. We'll be monitoring closely, and if we see any signs that things are going out of control, or that you're being harmed, we will intervene immediately."

Aidan nodded, feeling both a thrill of anticipation and a stab of trepidation at her words. He glanced at the plate in front of him, a hearty meal of fruits and grains that suddenly seemed like a last comfort before facing something unknown.

"Thank you, Ahlissa. I'm... prepared," he replied, though he wasn't entirely sure how true that was.

Ahlissa leaned back, her gaze drifting over the horizon. "The shard has proven unpredictable, and we've taken precautions to minimise any risks. But enough of that for now. You mentioned you visited the library in Cordovar - it's quite a sight inside, isn't it?"

"Yes," Aidan said, his eyes lighting up with genuine enthusiasm. "Very impressive. The archives are immense. I'm having a copy of a rare book made - *The Schism* - which I believe might have been written by your esteemed guest, Athovhar."

Ahlissa's eyebrows rose with interest. "Really? A strange coincidence, indeed. What led you to choose that one?"

"The topic covers historical tensions that may be relevant to the origins of the shard's magic," Aidan replied thoughtfully. "I also discovered something troubling. Apparently, the Council in Gideon is refusing requests for historical information."

Ahlissa frowned, exchanging a glance with Jillian. "No reason given?"

"None," Aidan answered, recalling his conversation with the library scholar. "It's almost like an embargo on knowledge. The scholar I spoke with seemed intrigued and baffled by it. This is recent, by all accounts."

"It's rare for Gideon's authorities to suppress accepted history," Ahlissa mused, swirling a spoon through her tea thoughtfully. "Did the scholar happen to mention when this censorship began?"

"It seems to have started just recently," Aidan confirmed.

Jillian looked uneasy, her brow furrowed. "It's strange, though. Gideon has always been known as a city that celebrates knowledge. Why impose restrictions on history now?"

Ahlissa gave a slow nod, her gaze distant. "Yes, very odd indeed. And concerning. History forms the foundation of a society's identity. If they're willing to manipulate that, what else might they be hiding? This sort of authoritarian shift... it reminds me of the old days in Kanarzand, when the Arcane Council decided what knowledge was 'acceptable' and what was too dangerous to be allowed."

Aidan's mouth tightened. "I fear that might be the influence of the Twelve. I've seen growing signs of Mhorvaeus's ties to their ranks. And, according to the library's archives, the Star Haunt - a place long rumoured to harbour dark secrets; was believed to be home to the Kale Khestari. Mhorvaeus seems to be orchestrating something larger than just a quest for power."

Ahlissa considered this, her fingers drumming lightly on the table. "Your former mentor, Professor Brevax, works with the council in Gideon, doesn't he?"

"Yes, and he's likely caught in the middle of this," Aidan replied. "The atmosphere in Cordovar was strange as well. A tabloid reporter managed to recognise me, and he asked probing questions about our activities."

Ahlissa groaned. "Oh no, not the tabloids again... Did they ask about me?"

Aidan smiled faintly. "Yes, they were clearly hoping to publish some scandalous story about us. I managed to redirect his attention by talking about my upcoming book instead. He seemed delighted with that lead and left with a flourish."

Ahlissa chuckled, relief mingling with a trace of annoyance. "The last thing we need is a public spectacle. Thank you for handling that. Hopefully, that's the last we'll hear from them for now."

They continued their breakfast in relative silence, the sky brightening as the Zephyr Breeze continued its course. After they'd finished, Jillian escorted Aidan to the shard's secure chamber, her gaze serious as they neared the door.

"Be careful," she murmured, her voice barely above a whisper. "And... good luck."

Aidan gave her a reassuring nod before stepping inside. The door closed behind him, leaving him alone with the shard. He could feel its presence, powerful and ancient, as if it were observing him even as he studied it.

The shard sat upon its pedestal, an amber crystal radiating a dark, inner light. Aidan's eyes were drawn to it, and he felt a faint tugging at the edges of his consciousness, almost as though it were calling to him. He took a deep breath and approached it, noting how the room seemed to dim as he drew closer, an illusion that made the shard appear to grow in size, towering over him.

This effect wasn't simply an illusion, he realised; it was an aura of dominance, an attempt by the shard to impose itself upon him. Aidan fought to clear his mind, resisting the influence, yet he couldn't deny the sensation that the shard was trying to reach him on a deeper level. His pulse quickened, but he steadied himself and extended a hand, fingertips brushing the cool, smooth surface of the amber crystal.

As he touched it, the shard's black veins began to pulse, dark symbols and arcane patterns shifting within its depths. They morphed before his eyes, rearranging into shapes he hadn't seen before, symbols that seemed to dance in and out of focus. He recognised elements of an ancient cuneiform, a form of ancient Sand Magic used for spells related to darkness, necromancy, and even demonology.

He had only glimpsed Sand Magic briefly in Kanarzand, and most scholars warned against delving into its darker applications. But here, in the presence of the shard, those forbidden spells came alive, whispering their secrets as if the shard itself were offering them to him.

Then he felt it; a presence, close, watching him. A shiver ran down his spine as he realised that this presence wasn't just from the shard's magic. There was something contained within it, something alive. He could feel it pulsing, breathing, waiting.

A living entity, he thought with a growing sense of horror. Not just any entity, but a demonic life force, a dark intelligence imprisoned within the shard, bound yet still conscious.

The name came to him then; *Qualtesh*. He could see it in his mind, an ancient city buried beneath the sands of the Forbidden Wastes, a place where the exiled Kale Ashtari had been banished. Images of a nightmarish landscape flashed through his mind, etched into his thoughts as though branded by fire. He felt the shard's will seeping into his own, urging him toward this cursed place.

73

"Go there," a voice commanded, echoing through his thoughts like a hiss. The shard seemed to vibrate with intensity, its pulse quickening.

Aidan tried to resist, but he felt himself succumbing to the power within the shard, his voice slipping into a whisper he could barely control. "Yes..."

The world around him went black.

When Aidan awoke, he was lying on a cot in the infirmary, a dull ache thudding through his head. He blinked, his vision coming into focus to see Jillian leaning over him, her face lined with worry. Beside her stood two Aystaran healers, their expressions unreadable but attentive.

"You collapsed again," Jillian informed him, her voice gentle but laced with concern. "Are you alright?"

Aidan nodded, trying to sit up. His mind swirled with fragments of what he had seen, pieces of dark knowledge that lingered in his thoughts. "There's... a demon imprisoned inside the shard," he said, his voice hoarse. "That's the presence I've been sensing. It's not just the magic; it's something alive. I saw visions... spells connected to Sand Magic, but a twisted, darker form. And I saw Qualtesh, a city buried beneath the sands. The demon... it wants to go there."

Jillian paled slightly, her fingers clutching the edge of his cot. "Then we're following the will of a demon? Aidan, this is dangerous. Demons manipulate and consume. This path; can we not turn back?"

Aidan shook his head, the weight of his realization pressing down on him. "It has a hold over me, Jillian. The connection we share... it's binding. And I think it's linked to my encounter at the Star Haunt. The demon has claimed me as its conduit. Even if we wanted to turn back, I don't think I could stop myself from trying to reach Qualtesh."

Jillian's face grew resolute, though a shadow of worry darkened her eyes. "We have to tell Ahlissa. If this journey is at the demon's bidding, then we're all in peril. My people have been seduced by such forces before, and the consequences were disastrous."

Aidan sighed, his hands clenching the edge of the cot. "I know. My intentions were pure, but I realize now that I'm putting everyone at risk. This quest; whatever hope I had of revealing a benign secret seems lost."

Jillian squeezed his arm, her touch gentle but firm. "When you're ready, let's talk to Ahlissa together. She needs to understand what we're up against."

Several hours passed before Aidan was well enough to leave his quarters. The ship glided through the night, the stars casting a soft, silvery glow over the deck as he waited in his cabin, contemplating the nightmarish implications of the shard's revelations. He wondered how something that had promised so much knowledge and power could mask such a dark truth.

Near midnight, a soft knock sounded on his door. Aidan opened it to find Ahlissa standing there, her expression grave yet sympathetic. "Penny for your thoughts?" she asked quietly. "I heard what happened."

Aidan gestured for her to come inside, then closed the door. He sank onto the edge of his bed, his head in his hands. "I can't believe how wrong I was," he murmured. "I thought this shard held secrets worth pursuing, but instead, it's led us to this."

Ahlissa sat down beside him, resting a hand on his shoulder. "Don't lose heart, Aidan. We all understood the risks when we agreed to join you on this journey into the Forbidden Wastes. Yes, this demon wants us to reach Qualtesh, but it's imprisoned within the shard. It can't act beyond it."

Aidan looked up at her, his face etched with worry. "But who imprisoned it, and why? Qualtesh... what is it about that place?"

Ahlissa's gaze drifted toward the window, where the faint light of dawn was beginning to touch the horizon. "That's something we'll have to uncover when we get there. I've already changed our course to avoid major cities, especially now that we know Mhorvaeus is watching us closely. We'll take a more discreet route, one that will frustrate his spies and hopefully keep us under the radar."

Aidan managed a faint smile. "You're always one step ahead."

Ahlissa returned his smile, her expression softening. "We suspected the shard was affecting you more than you realised. Athovhar sensed it, too, after speaking with you. It's clear now that this demon's influence is potent. We'll have to tread carefully but know this; you're not alone in this. We'll support you however we can."

He nodded, feeling a surge of gratitude despite the weight of his burden. "Thank you. Truly."

Ahlissa stood, brushing a hand through her hair. "Rest tonight, Aidan.

Tomorrow is a new day. I've accelerated the ship's speed, and by dawn, we should be stationed over Lake Glassmere. The beauty there might offer a welcome respite, even if only for a short time."

Aidan nodded, the promise of a new destination bringing a small spark of hope.

11

Lake Glassmere

Aidan awoke refreshed the next morning and immediately moved to the observation deck to see what was happening. The morning light filtered through the shimmering mists as the airship hovered over Lake Glassmere. A steady hum of activity filled the air.

Ahlissa stood there, speaking with a group of individuals whose distinct postures and animated conversation marked them as more than mere travellers. She turned and waved Aidan over with a smile.

"Aidan, it's time you met our reinforcements," she called, her voice carrying above the camp's din. "This is the team from the New Kanarzand Bureau of Archaeology. I pulled some strings to get them here."

As Aidan approached, Ahlissa began the introductions with a flourish.

"Draven Corviel, Lead Archaeologist and Expedition Leader," she said, gesturing toward a broad-shouldered man with dark hair streaked with silver. Draven's piercing gaze assessed Aidan like a freshly unearthed artefact. "We've heard a lot about you, Aidan. It's good to finally meet the man whose discoveries have caused quite a stir in our circles."

Aidan offered a firm handshake. "Your reputation precedes you, Draven. Glad to have your expertise."

Ahlissa motioned to the woman beside Draven, a petite figure with sharp eyes and an air of quiet confidence. "This is Elira Veylin, our resident Arcane Historian."

Elira inclined her head slightly, her arms crossed over a satchel brimming with scrolls. "I'm eager to see what mysteries this expedition uncovers. Particularly those runes you mentioned from Kale Khaestas. They intrigue me."

"Renlor Drax, Combat Historian," Ahlissa continued, nodding to a weathered man with a soldier's stance and a wary expression. "If trouble finds us, he'll keep us in one piece."

Renlor's handshake was brief and crushing. "Hope you know how to swing that sword of yours, Aidan. We might need it."

"Tessa Lorynth," Ahlissa said, introducing a vivacious woman who gave Aidan an enthusiastic grin. "She's our geomancer and a wizard with sand magic - literally."

"Wait until you see what I can do!" Tessa said brightly.

Finally, Ahlissa pointed to a tall, wiry man with a wild shock of hair. "And Malrik Fenhal, cryptozoologist and planar expert. He's as sharp as he is eccentric."

Malrik offered a theatrical bow. "Ah, a fellow seeker of mysteries! We'll make a fine team."

Aidan nodded, already sensing this group's skills would benefit the expedition.

As they moved deeper into the journey, Aidan's days turned to a meticulous blur of research and collaboration with the scholars and experts aboard the Zephyr Breeze.

Ahlissa had plotted their course to avoid major cities and towns, steering clear of watchful eyes and curious minds. They kept low to the rugged terrain by day and soared under cover of night, blending into the vast darkness. Aidan welcomed the work, diving head first into analysing the many documents and symbols they had collected. But even as he poured over the ancient texts, a persistent unease gnawed at him. Every time he slept, it was there, lurking.

It began subtly, just fragments of twisted landscapes and haunting whispers, but as they travelled closer to the Forbidden Wastes, the dreams morphed into full-fledged nightmares. His mind was yanked through dark realms, each vision more horrific than the last. In these visions, he saw the world through the eyes of some twisted, ancient entity, a malevolent presence that seemed to delight in chaos and torment. Its voice rasped at him from the shadows, the guttural tone echoing through his dreams like a claw raking through his thoughts. Every morning, he awoke drenched in sweat, heart pounding as if he had truly been there, enveloped in darkness.

Aidan spent countless hours in the ship's candle-lit study rooms with the scholars, piecing together fragments of information, hoping to uncover some clarity about the shard and the entity within it. But for all their efforts, the scholars remained perplexed. They knew the shard was an artefact from the Age of Darkness, a relic from an era buried in shadows and legends. Its inscriptions were written in a strange amalgamation of languages, with an unmistakable blend of Aystaran, Infernal, and even an ancient script tied to Sand Magic. This blend of languages defied standard translation, but Aidan's unique understanding of the symbols seemed to surprise the scholars.

As they poured over the meanings, symbols, and spells contained within the shard, it became evident to Aidan that the scholars couldn't truly decipher what he was seeing. Even when he explained it to them, their expressions remained blank. "It's as though it speaks only to him," one scholar murmured. They documented every detail, and while the shard's power was impressive, it left them all unsettled.

One day, as Aidan sat before the shard, tracing the symbols along its amber surface with a trembling finger, a word - a name - seared itself into his mind. It echoed like a chant in his thoughts, a name that carried a strange, forbidden power. He whispered it under his breath, then stopped, a jolt of fear washing over him. The scholars had explained to him the inherent danger in speaking the true names of certain beings. A name, if spoken in the wrong context, could act as a summoning or an anchor to the physical world. And something told Aidan that invoking this name would draw the entity within the shard dangerously close to the realm of the living.

After nearly a month and a half of navigating cautiously under night's cover, the Zephyr Breeze approached Lake Glassmere, a sprawling body of water glistening beneath the starlight. It connected multiple nations across Scylla; Scornland, Sindarr, Aden, Agaria, and the Aethyr Reaches.

From his perch on the observation deck, Aidan took in the view, grateful for a respite from the oppressive feeling the shard had been imposing on him.

The lake stretched endlessly, its dark waters swallowing the reflections of the stars above. On still nights, the lake was said to mirror the heavens so perfectly that it looked as though a second night sky lay below. Here, among the tranquil waters and sparse settlements dotting the shoreline, they were less likely to encounter spies or hostile agents. Still, Ahlissa remained cautious, instructing the crew to remain vigilant as they crossed into the Aethyr Reaches.

Over breakfast one morning, she briefed him and Jillian about their next phase. "Our path will take us over the Aethyr Reaches," she informed them, studying the map laid out before her. Her finger traced a route that curved around the northern edge of the lake, veering slightly south toward an isolated area marked only with the faint outline of hills and dark forests.

"Aethyr Reaches," Aidan repeated, mulling over the name. The region was unfamiliar to him, a swath of land rarely crossed by outsiders. It was known for its dense forests, magical creatures, and ancient druidic traditions, but he had heard only vague rumours of what lay within.

Ahlissa nodded, glancing up from the map. "The Reaches are sparsely populated, but it's not uninhabited. Druid sects and wild tribes hold sway there, and they keep a tenuous peace among the area's natural forces. Spirit creatures are rumoured to dwell deep in the forests, and while most are neutral or indifferent to travellers, we can't assume that will be the case. We'll need to avoid attracting the attention of certain groups."

"Certain groups?" Jillian asked, leaning forward with a curious expression.

"The Cult of the Dreaded Below," Ahlissa replied, her tone darkening. "They are a dark sect within the Reaches, known for worshipping an ancient entity said to slumber in the depths of the earth. The druids and wild tribes do what they can to keep the cult in check, but the Reaches are a dangerous place because of them. We'll avoid travelling directly over their known territories."

Aidan suppressed a shiver. The thought of encountering yet another dark force didn't sit well with him. He could still feel the shard's subtle pull, its influence gnawing at the edges of his consciousness even when he was awake. "Are there outposts or safe havens we can use for resupply?" he asked, glancing back down at the map.

"There are a few," Ahlissa said, tracing a spot near the border. "Two of the Aethyr Marked houses operate in this region; House Evarys and House Aaren. Evarys is skilled in Handling, mainly with magical creatures and elements, while Aaren deals in Trade. They keep outposts for travellers and are generally friendly to outsiders. We'll stop at one of these, briefly, for supplies."

Jillian pointed to a dark patch on the map, her brow furrowing. "And this place? It's marked with an eerie shading..."

Ahlissa's face grew serious. "That's the Shadow Wood; a forest where the trees are twisted and gnarled, as though the land itself were corrupted. Few dare to enter. Even the druids avoid it, believing the place to be haunted by ancient forces. Whatever dark magic warped that land has left a permanent stain."

Aidan felt his pulse quicken. The map's ominous details, combined with Ahlissa's warnings, painted the Aethyr Reaches as a place of wild, dangerous beauty. A place where the line between the natural world and the arcane blurred into something volatile and unpredictable. The journey was growing increasingly dangerous, and with each passing day, the shard's influence seemed to intensify, as though it knew they were drawing closer to its intended destination.

That night, as the Zephyr Breeze passed over the quiet forests of the Aethyr Reaches, Aidan lay in his cabin, struggling to quiet his mind. But sleep came, and with it, the dreams returned.

In the dream, he was standing on a barren, twisted landscape, a vast wasteland stretching in every direction. Shadows clung to the ground like mist, and strange shapes flickered at the edges of his vision, their forms just beyond comprehension. He turned, searching for an escape, but found only a dark, endless expanse.

A voice echoed through the void, deep and guttural, laced with malice. The name - the demon's name - resonated within him, growing louder with each repetition until it drowned out all other thoughts. He tried to cover his ears, but it was as if the sound came from within, pulsing through his veins, tearing at his mind.

"*Qualtesh...*" the voice whispered, laced with an ancient hunger. "*Come to me.*"

Aidan jolted awake, gasping for breath, his skin slick with sweat. His heart pounded in his chest as he sat up, clutching the blanket, his eyes darting around the dark cabin as if expecting to see the entity from his dreams standing there, waiting for him.

The voice lingered in his mind, its power echoing through him even in his waking state. He glanced over at his desk, where his notes on the shard lay scattered, and a shiver crept down his spine. The name Qualtesh was scrawled at the top of one page, his own handwriting a stark reminder of the visions haunting him.

Morning found Aidan bleary-eyed, but he forced himself to push through the exhaustion, returning to the study room to meet with the scholars. They continued to analyse the shard's patterns, tracing connections and attempting to unlock the spells hidden within. But with every new symbol Aidan deciphered, his unease grew. The spells were dark, sinister, meant for necromancy and binding, their power twisted by the influence of something infernal.

One scholar, a wiry man with a constant furrowed brow, looked up from the symbols, shaking his head. "This is ancient. A relic from the Age of Darkness. But why would anyone preserve such dark magic within a shard?"

"Because it's not just magic," Aidan replied, his voice quiet. "There's something in there; a demon, bound and imprisoned, but still conscious. And it's waiting for us to release it."

The scholars exchanged uneasy glances, their faces paling at his words. They had known the shard was dangerous, but this revelation added a new layer of horror.

"So... we're bringing it closer to freedom?" one of them whispered, his voice barely audible.

Aidan nodded grimly. "If we follow its guidance, it will lead us straight to its prison. It's using me as a conduit, feeding off my presence to grow stronger."

12

Breaching the Waste

The Zephyr Breeze coasted smoothly into the House Aaren outpost on the outskirts of Marthorn in the Aethyr Reaches, her sturdy hull gliding gracefully toward the dock. Constructed of timber and steel, the port was designed to blend seamlessly into the landscape, a mix of earthy greens and deep browns merging with the dense forest beyond. The structures of House Aaren - strong stone buildings with wood-beam facades and thick vines climbing the walls - stood beside the dock, their design in harmony with the surrounding wilderness to avoid disturbing the powerful natural magic of the druids.

Over two days, the crew of the Zephyr Breeze worked to restock supplies, gathering everything they would need for the perilous journey Northwest to the Forbidden Wastes. Ahlissa saw to business matters with her regular entourage of four crew members, while the others were granted shore leave, taking the chance to explore Marthorn.

Aidan and the Kale Khestari company, eager to stretch their legs after weeks aboard, ventured into the heart of the settlement. Marthorn's buildings were mostly low structures of timber and stone, designed with an eye for symmetry with the land. Tall, old trees lined the streets, and vines hung from the rooftops, providing shade and adding to the village's rustic beauty. Dirt tracks formed the primary paths between the buildings, with little separating the village from the surrounding fields and woodlands.

Aidan strolled through the town with a mix of curiosity and admiration. As he passed groups of locals, he noted how each person greeted him with a warm nod or a friendly smile. Jillian, who had joined him in exploring the area, pointed out the locals, whom she had learned were called "Reachers," individuals fiercely devoted to the land and its well-being.

"These people live simple lives, devoted to their families and their farms," Jillian explained as they observed the villagers tending to crop, livestock, and repair work. "They grow their own food, gather materials from the forest, and keep mostly to themselves. But there's a genuine warmth here; a sense of community."

Aidan nodded in agreement, feeling an odd sense of comfort in the village's peaceful atmosphere. In contrast to the looming journey ahead, Marthorn was a place where life moved at a slower pace, in harmony with the natural world. He and Jillian enjoyed a few hearty meals at the local inn, *The Whispering Tree*, where they were treated to rich stews, fresh bread, and a local ale that warmed the belly.

On the second day, they ventured into the forests beyond the village. Tall trees stretched overhead, filtering the sunlight into soft patches of gold and green that dappled the forest floor. The air was thick with the scent of pine and moss, and the sound of distant birdsong accompanied their steps. After a short walk, they came upon a small, clear pool fed by a gentle stream. Jillian knelt by the edge, dipping her toes into the cool water and closing her eyes with a smile.

"I've dreamt of such a place," she murmured, gazing at her reflection as it shimmered across the water's surface. "My homeland was ravaged by the Sah'ren, and nature was nearly wiped out in the process. To see such beauty... it's almost surreal."

Aidan watched her, struck by her sincerity and vulnerability. She turned to him, catching his gaze. "You're close to Ahlissa, aren't you?"

"No," he replied, shaking his head.

She looked at him thoughtfully, her expression soft. "A pity," she murmured, and before he could respond, she shrugged off her cloak, slipping into the pool without hesitation. The water glistened around her as she swam gracefully, a carefree smile on her lips. "This water is refreshing. Why don't you join me for a swim? Let go of the shard, the mission... just for a moment."

Aidan hesitated, then gave in, joining her in the pool. For the first time in what felt like weeks, he felt a strange lightness, a sense of freedom from the constant pressure and burden of the shard. The afternoon passed in laughter and easy conversation, a rare moment of peace amid the dark clouds gathering on the horizon of their mission.

The following morning, the crew returned to the ship, fully accounted for and ready to resume their journey. As the Zephyr Breeze took to the skies, they soared over the dense forests of the Aethyr Reaches, each mile bringing them closer to the treacherous expanse of the Forbidden Wastes. Ahlissa joined Aidan on the deck, pointing out the vast, untouched stretches of woodland below.

"All of this," she said, sweeping a hand across the vista, "was preserved after the Age of Calamity. Nations tried to claim it, to harness its power, but nature itself repelled them.

Eventually, they agreed to leave it to the druids, creating a separate nation where balance would be kept. It's a remarkable place, free from the hands of kings and conquerors."

Aidan took in the sight, marvelling at the beauty of the untouched land. But the further Northwest they travelled, the more the land below began to shift. Lush green forests gave way to cracked soil, dry rock, and patches of lifeless earth. The air grew colder, and a strange, foreboding energy filled the air.

A day passed, and then, rising like a dark wall across the horizon, the Stormcrags loomed before them. The jagged mountains were vast and foreboding, their peaks lost in swirling clouds that seemed to glow with hidden lightning.

"The Stormcrags," Ahlissa announced. "This range forms a natural barrier to the Forbidden Wastes. We have two choices: follow the range north or south to find a pass, or fly over them, risking the violent storms that have torn many ships to pieces."

Aidan peered at the churning clouds that shrouded the peaks, the occasional flash of lightning illuminating the sharp ridges. "Isn't there a way to calm the storms? With magic?"

Ahlissa shook her head. "The storms here are ancient and unpredictable.

Attempting to control them would require powerful magic and could backfire catastrophically. The air will thin at higher altitudes, which might affect our wits when we need them most."

She directed the crew to search for a rumoured gap in the range. It was a dangerous path, where the cliffs closed in tightly on both sides, leaving only a narrow channel for them to navigate. Cautiously, they guided the ship into the passage. Rock walls rose steeply around them, casting shadows over the ship as it glided through. The slightest miscalculation could mean disaster, but Ahlissa's skilled navigation kept them on course.

After two tense hours, they emerged on the other side of the range, and a bleak, desolate landscape stretched out before them. The ground below was cracked and barren, a place devoid of life, and a dust storm churned in the distance, a dark, roiling mass that swept across the horizon.

As Ahlissa issued commands for the crew to assess the ship's condition, a crew member reported a malfunction in their navigational equipment. "The landscape here is highly magnetized," he explained. "It's affecting our ability to detect landmarks or incoming threats."

"Switch to visual navigation," Ahlissa ordered calmly. "We'll fly lower and rely on sight."

Aidan offered to map the terrain as they travelled, and Ahlissa agreed, recognizing the value of having a first hand record of their journey through these hostile lands. But even as they continued, the dust storm they had spotted earlier began to sweep closer, growing larger and darker until it filled the sky ahead.

"We won't outrun that," Ahlissa said grimly. "Prepare for impact and shield the ship."

Within minutes, the storm was upon them. Winds howled, and sand battered the hull like shards of glass. Visibility dropped to near zero, and the ship's shields hummed as they absorbed the relentless force of the sand. Aidan felt light-headed, a sensation that lingered even after he drank water Jillian handed him, a concerned frown on her face.

The burning sensation flared again along his lower back, followed by a whisper; a voice so faint he almost missed it. But the voice was familiar, ominous, and brought with it a wave of disorientation.

"Izen'draazt," he murmured, the name slipping from his lips as he struggled to regain his focus.

Jillian reached over, touching his arm with a look of alarm. "Stay still," she whispered, and gently examined his back, but she found nothing amiss. "Your obsession with the shard... I think it's drawing something to you," she said, worry lining her face.

Just then, a warning blared from the deck. The crew scrambled as two ships appeared from the murky haze ahead, their hulking forms twisted and dark. They were ghastly vessels, built from what appeared to be bones, wood, and steel, shaped like massive skeletal beasts, with red shields glowing around their hulls. Each ship was armed with rows of ballistae and thick grappling hooks.

Ahlissa grabbed her eyepiece, examining the ships as they approached. "Argar ships," she muttered. "They're flying the mark of Kazum Dra. Prepare for combat."

An incoming communication crackled over the speakers, a deep, guttural voice cutting through the static. "Enemy vessel, you have entered the domain of Kazum Dra. I am Captain Cortesh of the Alqabda. Surrender your ship or be destroyed."

Ahlissa's eyes flashed with defiance. "Put me through," she instructed, then replied, "Captain Cortesh, today is not your day. Stand down, or you'll regret crossing paths with us."

She turned to the crew. "Battle stations. Prepare to fire."

The two enemy ships manoeuvred into attack position, ballistae gleaming with sharpened bolts aimed at the Zephyr Breeze. Ahlissa wasted no time, ordering the gunners to open fire. A broadside of incendiary shells exploded from their cannons, tearing into the nearest ship and setting its deck ablaze.

The enemy retaliated, firing their ballistae, and the Zephyr Breeze shook as bolts thudded into its side. A few struck the shield, ricocheting off in showers of sparks. Aidan braced himself as the ship veered, swinging to face the second vessel, which climbed above them, firing grapple lines down onto the deck.

"Prepare to repel boarders!" Ahlissa shouted as the enemy lines hit the deck. Argar raiders slid down the ropes, leaping onto the deck with weapons drawn. Aidan's hand instinctively went to his sword, and he drew it as Jillian appeared beside him, her scimitars blazing with energy.

A half-Argar raider with a wicked-looking axe lunged at him, but Aidan dodged, swinging his blade in a swift arc that left a deep gash across the creature's side. Enraged, the half-Argar swung back, narrowly missing Aidan's head. Aidan struck again, this time piercing the raider's leather armour, and the creature collapsed with a snarl.

Nearby, Jillian fought with agility and precision, cutting down Argar raiders as they swarmed her, but more kept coming. Aidan leapt to her side, dispatching another raider before they could reach her.

Suddenly, a blast of fireballs erupted from the enemy ship, hammering the Zephyr Breeze in a furious assault. Aidan and Jillian dove for cover as the fireballs exploded around them, the shield struggling to hold back the flames. The sky darkened as a swarm of shadowy, winged creatures emerged from the enemy vessel, swarming over the Zephyr Breeze.

Aidan felt a strange surge within him, a burning energy that heightened his senses. He stood, casting a powerful Wind Storm down the corridor where the creatures had swarmed, flinging them back and smashing them against the walls. The crew quickly finished off the stunned creatures, and the swarm dissipated, their bodies evaporating into smoke.

Ahlissa, standing resolute on the command deck, ordered a final cannon volley. The powerful blast tore through the second enemy vessel, splintering it to pieces, and the fragments disappeared into the storm below.

As the last of the enemy was cleared from the ship, Aidan felt a strange calm settle over him. Exhausted but triumphant, he joined Jillian and Ahlissa as they assessed the damage.

"That was a bit of fun, wasn't it?" Ahlissa said, a spark of pride in her eyes. "We'll rest here for now, take shelter in the rock formations below and assess the hull. You did well out there, Aidan. I think this journey is awakening something within you."

13

The Labyrinth

The Zephyr Breeze shuddered as it drifted into the cavernous crevice, the airship's shield fluctuating wildly under the strain of the raging storm. As the howling winds diminished, the crew let out collective sighs of relief. After days of navigating fierce weather and attacks, Ahlissa's crew were visibly worn, and the damaged hull and strained shielding systems hinted at the toll the journey had taken.

"Battle damage report!" Ahlissa barked, moving across the bridge with an air of command. Her voice rang with resolve, but Aidan saw the concern shadowing her eyes as she awaited the crew's assessments.

"Four wounded," came a terse reply from a crew member holding a stained rag against his forehead, "Hull breaches below on Decks Two and Three, and the shard energy's depleting faster than expected, Captain. Morale... the men are uneasy."

Ahlissa took this in stride, her expression impassive, and turned to Aidan. "We'll remain here until repairs are completed and the storm subsides. The crew need rest, and I need you ready for whatever lies ahead." Her eyes held a strange glint. "Jillian tells me you handled yourself exceptionally well in the skirmish. She saw abilities in you that even you may have doubted existed."

Aidan shifted under her gaze, feeling an unexpected warmth in her praise. "It felt different. It was as though the Aethyr Mark; whatever it is; helped me, gave me strength."

Ahlissa nodded thoughtfully. "It's rare to see an Aethyr Mark manifest in such a way, especially one that offers powers beyond mere skill. You know the Twelve would mark you as deviant if they saw it, but rest assured, so long as I am Captain, no such harm will come to you."

"I appreciate that," he replied, feeling a hint of apprehension at the thought of his strange new mark and its implications. "And I'm prepared for what that means. If it's ever dangerous to you, I'll take responsibility."

Ahlissa's hand rested briefly on his shoulder. "We're all in this together, Aidan. Your fate is intertwined with ours now."

With that, she turned to oversee the repair efforts, her confident strides a reassurance to all who watched her. Aidan, feeling the weight of her trust, moved to the lower decks where he found Jillian, who was mending the damaged hull alongside two crew members. To his surprise, Jillian was working her craft with an ease and precision that he hadn't fully appreciated until now.

"Aidan!" she greeted him, wiping her brow but beaming. "Your timing is perfect. Hold this here, would you?"

He stepped forward, bracing the wood against the hull as Jillian conjured fasteners using magic he hadn't seen her employ before. Energy flowed from her hands into the material, her concentration unwavering. "I must say, Jillian, you make magic look effortless," he said, unable to hide his admiration.

She chuckled, casting him a sideways glance. "Thank you, Aidan. I'm glad to surprise you once in a while. And you... you held your own. You looked almost as at home with that sword as I do with these spells."

They worked together in comfortable silence, exchanging glances and smiles as they fortified the hull. When the repair was done, they found a quiet corner and sat, fatigue etched into their faces.

"I suppose I owe you some explanation," Jillian said, crossing her legs and folding her hands in her lap. "You know I'm Khystar, and my people... well, we have some unusual abilities." She summoned a shimmering scimitar from thin air, watching the magical weapon sparkle for a moment before releasing it. "It's like breathing to me, Aidan. My armour, my weapons... they're as much a part of me as my own skin."

Aidan nodded, a grin creeping onto his face. "Well, it suits you. You looked formidable, even graceful out there."

She raised a brow, her lips curving into a smirk. "Thank you. Not bad yourself; for a scholar who'd rather be surrounded by scrolls. Just don't make me expect that level of bravery every day," she teased, nudging his arm.

They exchanged quiet laughs, their voices mingling with the distant rumble of the storm above, and for a while, they spoke of lighter things, tales from their homelands, and dreams of simpler lives. As they retired to their quarters, Aidan felt a rare sense of peace, a lull before the inevitable storm that lay beyond the craggy shelter.

* * *

Late into the evening, Aidan was awoken by a firm knock on his door. Blinking the sleep from his eyes, he pulled on his robe and opened it to find one of Ahlissa's crew waiting.

"The representative of Kale Ereshkigal requests your presence," the man informed him, bowing with a respectful nod.

Adjusting his robes, Aidan followed the crew member down the cold, narrow corridors to Athovhar's chambers. As he approached, the air turned sharply colder, a chill settling in his bones. The door opened as he neared, revealing the stately form of the Deathless One, clad in robes of silver and sapphire, his gaze piercing and unyielding.

"We meet again, Aidan," Athovhar said in his calm, measured tone. "Ahlissa has told me of your valour in the recent battle. It seems that the blood of the Kale Khestari flows within you."

Aidan dipped his head respectfully. "It felt... like something in me awakened, perhaps my Aethyr Mark," he said, pausing as he weighed his words. "It empowered me."

Athovhar studied him closely, his ageless eyes narrowing slightly. "Indeed. Some marks are more than mere adornments. They draw from deeper forces, both within and beyond. Tell me, what do you know

99

of the Forbidden Wastes?"

"Only fragments," Aidan admitted, recalling his studies. "The Kale Ashtari once lived here, their city lost to ruin. I encountered what may have been one of their outposts; the Star Haunt; and I suspect that the demon Izen'draazt is connected to them somehow."

Athovhar nodded slowly. "The Kale Ashtari were indeed a splinter of the Khestar, driven underground and transformed in the abyss. They wielded dark Aethyr, abandoning the light to survive in those twisted realms. But Qualtesh is different. Its fall left scars that run deep into the underworld itself, an evil that pulls at the souls of any who enter its domain."

Athovhar's gaze grew steely. "Know this, Aidan. The dark energies of the Forbidden Wastes hold sway over those who enter, tempting them to lose themselves. Qualtesh will bind your mind, erode your spirit, and prey on the darkness in your soul. To survive it... you must not surrender yourself to its shadows."

Aidan took in the warning, feeling a shiver run down his spine. "What of my Aethyr Mark? Could it draw me further into that darkness?"

The Deathless One's eyes softened briefly. "Your mark feeds on fear and shadows, I sense that. But its true nature lies not in evil; it is in your choices. The mark binds you to forces far older than Scylla itself, and yes, perhaps Izen'draazt has found a way to exploit that connection. But your will remains your own. Resist the demon's lure, and you will keep your soul."

As Athovhar spoke, Aidan felt the burden of his fate settle heavily upon him. He was caught between two worlds; the scholar who sought knowledge and the warrior marked by ancient power, pursued by the shadows of his own past. Yet the Deathless One's assurance gave him a glimmer of hope, a lifeline in the dark.

"Thank you, Athovhar," he said, bowing his head. "I will heed your words."

Athovhar's expression softened, almost imperceptibly. "Rest now, Aidan. There is still much that lies ahead, and you will need all your strength."

* * *

That night, as the storm raged outside, Aidan lay restless in his quarters, turning over the events of the day in his mind. He tossed and turned, haunted by a sensation that something was drawing closer. A sudden burning erupted across his lower back, like searing brands being etched into his skin.

Gasping in pain, he stumbled to the mirror, pulling back his tunic to see a dark, twisting mark forming over his spine. It writhed and shifted beneath his skin, its serpentine coils seeming to pulse with a hungry life of their own. Aidan clenched his fists, struggling to keep calm as the mark settled, its shape resembling the symbols he'd seen at the Star Haunt.

As the pain faded, he noticed something strange; the minor disfigurements he had carried since the tainting had vanished, his skin smooth and his complexion clearer. The mark seemed to have absorbed the darkness within him, feeding on it like a parasitic creature.

Unable to shake his alarm, he left his quarters and sought out Ahlissa, finding her in her private quarters. When she opened the door, her eyes widened at the sight of him, clearly sensing his distress.

"Ahlissa... it's happened," he whispered, recounting the strange emergence of his mark. "It feeds on dark energy. It... it consumed my taint."

She listened in silence, then stepped closer, examining the mark on his back with a practiced eye. Her fingers traced the lines of the shifting tattoo, her brow furrowed. "This is... extraordinary," she said, her voice tinged with both awe and apprehension. "It's unlike any Aethyr Mark I've seen. The Twelve would have branded you deviant instantly."

"Then let's keep this secret," Aidan replied, his voice low. "If it were known... I'd be hunted."

Ahlissa nodded, meeting his gaze with a fierce loyalty. "Your secret is safe with me. But I suggest you keep an eye on this mark. If it hungers for dark energy, the Forbidden Wastes may offer more than it needs."

* * *

The next day, the Zephyr Breeze emerged from the cavern, gliding over a blasted landscape of cracked earth, barren rock, and rivers of molten lava. Ahlissa pointed northward, her gaze sharp. "We'll avoid Kazum Dra and find a way through the Labyrinth. It's dangerous, but if Qualtesh exists, it lies within these chasms."

Aidan joined her on the bridge, noting the bleak, hellish expanse stretching out before them. Jillian, who had joined them, shivered, her eyes wide as she looked upon the desolation below.

"This place... it's as if the land itself despises life," she whispered, clutching her arms. "I've seen horrors before, but nothing like this. I fear... I fear this wasteland will consume us."

Aidan placed a comforting hand on her shoulder. "We're here together, Jillian. We'll find Qualtesh, and we'll leave this place behind."

Ahlissa's voice broke through their quiet exchange, her tone resolute. "Let's be swift. I'd rather not linger in this cursed land longer than we must."

* * *

Hours passed as the Zephyr Breeze wound its way through the vast chasms and shadowy canyons of the Labyrinth. The cliffs loomed tall on either side, the eerie sounds of distant wails and the faint smell of sulphur filling the air. Occasionally, they glimpsed strange shadows flitting through the rocky maze, but none dared approach the airship.

Then, as dusk fell, a new threat appeared on the horizon; two skeletal airships, their frames glowing red against the darkening sky. Ahlissa cursed under her breath, issuing swift commands to the crew. "Outrun them," she ordered, her voice tense. "We can't afford another fight here."

With a surge of power, the Zephyr Breeze accelerated, leaving the skeletal ships trailing behind. The crew breathed a sigh of relief as their pursuers vanished into the distance, their figures swallowed by the misty twilight.

As the night descended, Aidan and Jillian shared a quiet moment on the deck. Aidan showed her the mark that had appeared on his back, and she looked at him with a mixture of awe and worry.

"This... this feels like the hold of the Sah'ren over my people," she whispered, her eyes reflecting a sadness he hadn't seen before. "I fear for you, Aidan. I would hate to see you consumed by such a mark."

He took her hand, offering a reassuring squeeze. "I won't be. Athovhar believes it doesn't control me, and I trust his wisdom."

Her fingers tightened around his. "Then I'll trust it too. Just... don't let it take you from me."

They held each other's gaze, a silent understanding passing between them as the ship drifted deeper into the shadows of the Labyrinth. The air grew colder, the darkness more oppressive, but in that quiet moment, Aidan felt a renewed strength; a resolve to see this journey through, for all their sakes.

14

Entering the Rift

For seven gruelling days, the Zephyr Breeze prowled the bleak and twisted landscape of the Forbidden Wastes, its crew ever alert, scanning the scorched earth and shadowed cliffs for any sign of a lost city. At last, Aidan felt it; a pull so powerful, so certain, that it was like a hand guiding him toward a dark maw in the earth, hidden amidst jagged rocks and twisted remnants of long-dead trees. He turned to Ahlissa, his eyes filled with conviction.

"Down there," he said, gesturing toward the gaping chasm. "That's where we need to go."

Ahlissa's gaze followed his, and she nodded. With a swift command, she directed her crew to bring the ship down into the cavernous opening. As the airship descended, magical light beacons flared to life, casting an eerie glow across the stony walls, illuminating strange shadows that slithered into dark crevices and disappeared as the lights swept across them.

Inside the cavern, the Zephyr Breeze glided carefully along a vast, yawning tunnel. For nearly two miles, the passage stretched on, the dimensions grand enough to accommodate their vessel. But as they progressed deeper, the tunnel narrowed, the walls pressing in, the roof dipping lower. At a point where the crevices narrowed too dangerously, Ahlissa made the call.

"We can't risk going further. We'll make camp here," she commanded. Her voice echoed off the cavern walls as the crew began preparations, unloading equipment, erecting tents, and establishing defensive perimeters.

Aidan, Jillian, and a few others scouted the immediate area. They found the crumbling remains of ancient buildings; weathered stone structures collapsed into ruin, but still whispering of a time when people had dwelt here. Dust and rubble covered the cracked remnants of walls, floors littered with fragments of long-forgotten artefacts.

Inscriptions, barely visible on the fractured stones, caught Aidan's eye. He brushed away layers of dirt, revealing faded, carved words.

"A bastion of hope and light among the dark and unliving," he read aloud, his voice tinged with awe. He continued deciphering fragments: "The path of light was lost to us... we will again rise to reclaim our true world... we are lost to our brothers, our kin of the surface world."

Ahlissa appeared beside him, studying the ruins thoughtfully. "Could this be the entrance to Qualtesh?"

Aidan nodded slowly. "The architecture is ancient enough. This could be part of a settlement, or maybe even an outpost leading to the city."

"Then we're on the right track," she replied, satisfied. "We'll make this our base camp, then. From here, we'll push forward into the depths."

As the crew assembled their camp, the Kale Khestari warriors took positions around the perimeter, weapons at the ready, their watchful eyes scanning the dark reaches of the cavern. The feeling of foreboding that had settled over them since entering the Wastes intensified, the walls seeming to close in, shadows deepening with every flicker of their torches. They took shifts, guarding their position as they prepared for the exploration ahead.

* * *

With the initial camp established, the party - comprising Ahlissa, Jillian, Aidan, a detachment of Kale Khestari warriors, two Aystaran mages, a priest, the experts from the New Kanarzand Bureau of Forbidden Archaeology and several crew members - ventured deeper into the darkness. The cavern gave way to an ancient, rocky passage that gradually transformed into man-made stonework: pillars, now little more than crumbling remnants, lined the path, and fragments of old paving stones lay scattered underfoot, a testament to a lost civilisation.

The deeper they went, the more oppressive the air became, the silence punctuated by the faintest scuffling noises that echoed ominously through the tunnel. The warriors fanned out, forming a protective perimeter, their eyes darting to every shadow, every dark corner.

Then, suddenly, a shout rang out; a scream of horror. Aidan spun toward the sound, only to see a figure disappearing into the darkness above, yanked violently off the ground by something unseen.

"Take cover!" the commander shouted, his voice ringing with urgency. "Shields up!"

Before they could fully react, two more warriors were seized, snatched by monstrous forms lurking in the shadows above. The Aystaran mages raised their hands, casting a series of light spells that burst across the cavern ceiling, illuminating a sight that sent a chill through everyone present.

Suspended above them, skittering on webs that clung to the cavern's vaulted heights, were spiders; enormous creatures with bloated, mottled bodies and too many eyes that gleamed in the harsh light. Their twisted legs, tipped with cruel spines, gripped the stone as they crawled across the ceiling with terrifying speed. At the mages' light, some scattered, but three dropped down with a thud, their legs flexing as they prepared to strike.

Jillian's armour shimmered into being around her, a sleek Aystaran battle suit that crackled with power. Energy swords formed in her hands, their radiant light casting a sharp gleam over her determined expression as she stepped forward, ready to engage.

The spiders moved quickly, closing the distance. One surged toward a warrior, who raised his spear just as the creature lunged. Its mandibles clamped onto his arm, and a horrified scream echoed as venom surged into his veins. The man fell, writhing in agony.

Ahlissa's voice rang out. "Defensive formation! Shields and spears at the ready!"

The Kale Khestari warriors obeyed instantly, forming a tight circle as they raised their shields and levelled their spears. The spiders hissed, their dark eyes reflecting the light with a cold, empty malice as they advanced.

Aidan felt the weight of something sinister close by. A scraping sound from the rocks drew his gaze, and he spun to see one of the massive arachnids crawling toward him, its mandibles clacking, eyes fixed hungrily on him. Without hesitation, Aidan drew an arrow, igniting it with a quick spell before unleashing it toward the creature. The flaming arrow struck true, embedding itself in the spider's grotesque head. The creature recoiled, letting out a screech of pain, but it pressed forward, undeterred.

As it closed in, Aidan had no time to draw another arrow. He dropped his bow and pulled out his sword, bracing himself as the creature lunged. Its mandibles sank into his shoulder, a burning pain flooding through him as venom laced into his bloodstream. Aidan gritted his teeth, pushing back the dizzying sensation that threatened to overwhelm him. With a surge of determination, he swung his blade, striking the spider across its face.

The creature reared back, hissing, but struck again, trying to wrap its spindly legs around him and pull him close to its spined body. Aidan twisted free, narrowly dodging its lethal embrace, and delivered a quick succession of strikes to its head. Finally, with a final, forceful blow, he drove his sword deep into its grotesque eyes. The spider let out a chittering, dying screech before collapsing at his feet, its body twitching in death.

He looked around, heart pounding, to see that the battle was still raging. Jillian fought with deadly efficiency, her energy swords flashing as she engaged two spiders at once, her movements swift and precise. One spider lunged at her, but she ducked, slicing through its legs in a smooth, fluid motion. Her eyes gleamed with determination as she leaped forward, plunging her swords into its body and finishing it off.

The mages, too, were not idle. They cast fireballs that exploded against the spiders with devastating effect, searing their bodies and driving the remaining creatures back into the shadows. After a few more moments of fierce combat, the remaining spiders skittered up the walls, vanishing into the dark crevices above.

The dust settled, and Ahlissa quickly took stock of the situation. Two warriors lay on the ground, unconscious but alive, their faces pale and sweat-soaked from the effects of the venom. Aidan approached as Malrik Fenhal, the cryptozoologist, inspected the fallen spiders, prodding at their bodies with a cautious curiosity.

"These are not ordinary spiders," Malrik said, his voice tinged with alarm. "The venom is potent, inducing a disorienting effect that can kill if untreated. Has anyone been bitten?"

Aidan raised a hand, wincing at the lingering pain in his shoulder. "I managed to resist it, but... it's unpleasant."

Malrik handed him a vial filled with a swirling, silver liquid. "Drink this, just to be sure."

He drank the potion, feeling a cooling sensation spread through his body as the antidote took effect. Around him, the mages treated the wounded warriors, reviving them with neutralizing salves and potions. Slowly, colour returned to the men's faces, and they blinked groggily as they were helped to their feet.

As the group regrouped, the oppressive darkness around them seemed to deepen. A palpable sense of dread filled the air, settling heavily over them. The mages exchanged wary glances, their faces shadowed with concern.

"We sense something... sinister," one of them said, her voice low and grim. "This place is saturated with Dark Aethyr. The closer we go, the greater the risk that we will fall under its influence. This is not merely an abandoned city; it's a place of death."

Aidan felt a cold shiver crawl down his spine. As they ventured further, he'd noticed subtle changes in himself; a faint, creeping sensation of despair, a dullness in his vision, as though the colour was being leeched from the world. And there were voices, faint whispers at the edge of his mind, snarling and hissing in a language he couldn't understand.

Ahlissa's gaze hardened as she listened. "If any of us succumb to this influence, it will show," she said firmly. "The mages tell me that an affected individual will begin to fade, becoming less visible to us, as though they are... crossing over."

Aidan swallowed, the weight of her words settling over him like a shroud. They were venturing into a realm where the boundary between life and death was thin, where darkness called out to the living, seeking to claim their souls. He steeled himself, knowing that their journey was only beginning, and that whatever waited in the depths of Qualtesh would test them in ways he could barely imagine.

* * *

After a brief rest, they pressed onward, the ancient stonework beneath their feet giving way to a vast, crumbling stairway. Pillars lay shattered on either side, twisted and broken as though by some great force. They descended cautiously, the walls pressing close, the air thick with a sense of foreboding.

Suddenly, the faint scuttling noise returned, echoing from somewhere beyond their line of sight. Aidan's hand tightened on his sword, his senses heightened as he scanned the shadows. He felt the pull of the Aethyr Mark on his back, tingling, like an instinct warning him of imminent danger.

They had barely reached the bottom of the stairway when the darkness above stirred. Shapes moved; a multitude of shadows, a wave of skittering legs and clicking mandibles. More spiders, and behind them, larger figures, monstrous amalgamations of flesh and shadow, their forms shifting as they advanced.

Ahlissa raised her sword, her voice ringing out clear and defiant. "Defensive positions! Hold the line!"

The Kale Khestari warriors tightened their formation, their faces resolute as the horde bore down upon them. Aidan felt the fire of the Aethyr Mark flare to life within him, filling him with a fierce resolve. Whatever awaited them in the depths, he would face it head-on. Together, they would carve a path through the darkness or fall in defiance of the evil that lurked within the heart of Qualtesh.

With a deep breath, Aidan braced himself as the creatures closed in, his sword raised and ready, his eyes locked on the shadows ahead.

The creatures surged forward, their grotesque forms a wave of darkness and malice, closing the distance with chilling speed. Aidan swung his sword in sweeping arcs, the blade's edge catching the pale light of the mage's spells that flickered desperately around them. The Kale Khestari warriors fought with ferocity, fending off the onslaught with disciplined precision. Jillian, her twin energy blades humming, struck at the monsters' limbs, carving a protective path around Aidan and the others. For a time, it seemed they might hold their ground.

Yet, for every creature they felled, two more crawled from the shadows, drawn by some unseen force from the depths. Ahlissa's voice rang out over the chaotic clash of steel and chitin. "Fall back! Regroup by the main passage!"

They retreated, striking down the relentless creatures as they withdrew toward a narrow, winding path that led deeper into the heart of the cavern. As they cleared the last creature from their immediate path, the group stumbled into a vast opening. Aidan's gaze fell upon an ancient gateway, crumbling and half-buried in rock. Strange symbols were carved along its archway, radiating an eerie light that seemed to beckon them forward.

"Qualtesh," Aidan murmured, realising they had uncovered the entrance to the lost city.

15

Qualtesh

Aidan, Jillian, Ahlissa, the specialists, and the Kale Khestari warriors pressed deeper into the twisting underground passages. The path was a disorienting descent, taking them further from the surface and into the depths of Scylla's underworld, where time and light seemed to hold no sway. As they moved, the air grew thick, warm, and damp, carrying the faint but unsettling tang of decay. Occasionally, the ground trembled, sending a low rumble that seemed to reverberate through the very bones of the earth. Even the hardened Kale Khestari grew solemn as the journey stretched on, none of them able to shake a sense of dread that pressed in closer with each step.

Nothing lived here. The lifeless silence only heightened the unease that clung to them, and for four days, they wandered down this abyssal path, resting only briefly before continuing on. At last, they arrived at a vast ledge that opened onto a breathtaking expanse, though any awe quickly gave way to horror. In the distance, a thundering river poured from a gap in the stone, its waters plunging into an endless black chasm below, while an eerie, unsettling darkness devoured the cavern around it.

Aidan's gaze followed the scouts as they scoured the nearby ledges for any sign of the ancient city they sought. "Signs of a road here," one of the scouts called back. "And remains of statues along the edge."

Approaching, Aidan saw the shattered statues – once giant monoliths that had crumbled to piles of rubble. Alongside the ruins, he uncovered a faintly familiar face carved in the weathered stone: Aystaran, yet unmistakably different. The figure's ears bore an extra point, one that suggested an evolution – or corruption – of what might once have been Aystaran.

"Could this be the face of the Kale Ashtari?" Ahlissa mused, running a hand across the stone face in reverence. The weathered lines seemed to tell a story, one etched by centuries of isolation and despair.

Aidan nodded. "The vision I saw at Star Haunt held faces like these. We're close to finding Qualtesh, I can feel it."

Jillian said little but gazed thoughtfully at the features of the crumbled statues. Her eyes held a flicker of understanding – or perhaps recognition – before she fell back into silence.

The shattered road continued onward, spiralling downwards along a ledge that hugged the cavern's walls. Ancient gatehouses and fragments of towering stone blocks hinted at a massive wall that had once protected these lands, but nothing remained intact. Aidan deciphered fragments of text from the scattered stones, noting with wonder that, while written in an archaic script, the language bore striking similarities to Aystaran.

"This is Qualtesh. Our home beneath home. Always. We are lost from

the Light," he read aloud, piecing together the phrase from different fragments.

A chill ran down Jillian's spine. "Lost from the Light... What a grim fate."

"It's as if they accepted their isolation," Aidan added, scanning the inscriptions. "This was more than just exile. It was a surrender."

The words seemed to resonate with the quiet sadness hanging over the ruins, stirring whispers among the scholars and Kale Khestari. The Aystaran mages, however, looked perturbed, sensing a disturbing energy that seemed to press in closer the further they ventured. One of the priests conferred with Ahlissa, sharing their concerns in hushed tones.

"Our powers are waning here," he warned her. "If we go much deeper, we might find ourselves without any protection."

Ahlissa acknowledged their words with a nod. "Thank you. We'll remain vigilant."

They continued, descending further until the cavern wall opened to reveal the sprawling ruins of the city of Qualtesh. Dark, silent, and grand in its decay, the city stretched across the abyss. Crumbling buildings, streets choked with ancient rubble, and dark, twisted statues loomed in the darkness, casting long shadows that seemed to dance in the flickering torchlight.

"We've arrived," Ahlissa announced softly, as if unwilling to disturb the dead.

Aidan, feeling an intense pull from somewhere deep within the ruins, instructed the scouts to search for a defensible position to set up camp. The scouts located an old stone house, its structure partially intact, enough to offer shelter for the night. As they settled in, Aidan felt an oppressive, watchful presence settle over him. It prickled at his senses, filling him with an inexplicable dread.

"I feel we're being watched," he murmured to Ahlissa and Jillian. "Something malevolent."

Ahlissa scanned the shadows warily. "Nobody should venture alone here," she instructed, her voice grave.

Later, while the camp settled, a peculiar discovery was made. Among the rubble, they unearthed a rusted metal panel bearing the words "Platform One."

"That's... unusual," Ahlissa said, her brow furrowed. "I've only seen similar markings at Platform Nine near Kanarzand. One group managed to activate it, and I suspect it played a part in Kanarzand's fate."

Aidan thought back to the Star Haunt, but this place felt different; older, darker. There was a pervasive energy here that gnawed at him, resonating with the Aethyr Mark that had recently manifested on his skin, a constant, sinister reminder of Izen'draazt's grip.

The following morning, scouts reported spotting a temple built into the cavern wall. At Aidan's suggestion, the group crossed into the temple grounds, traversing broken bridges over narrow canals and shattered archways. When they reached the towering double doors of the temple, partially open and looming forty feet above them, Aidan felt the dark presence intensify. It pressed into him like a weight, filling his mind with whispers and faint, mocking laughter.

"We'll be ready for anything," Ahlissa reassured him, though her expression betrayed her own unease.

"I fear there may be a guardian here," Aidan said. "If so, it will most likely be corrupted." He steeled himself, gripping the hilt of his sword tightly. "If that happens, I may need you all to pull back."

The group entered the courtyard, its flagstones cracked and littered with bones. Suddenly, a brilliant flash blinded Aidan. He felt his knees buckle, his vision clouded by a vivid hallucination of the past: the courtyard was filled with the lost citizens of Qualtesh, their faces twisted by the corrupting taint of darkness. Aidan's heart pounded as he recognised them from his vision; priests, acolytes, and nobles, each bearing symbols matching the Aethyr Mark now inscribed on his back.

The vision faded, leaving him on his knees in the present. Jillian crouched beside him, worry etched across her face. "Aidan! Are you all right?"

He nodded shakily, recounting the vision to them. "I believe these people were already succumbing to darkness even before their fall."

Inside the temple's main hall, they found further remnants of a fallen society. Stone pews lay overturned, bones scattered haphazardly on the ground. The walls were lined with engravings, bearing the same marks that appeared on Aidan's Aethyr Mark.

"Aidan," Ahlissa urged, noticing his drawn expression. "Anything here feel... familiar?"

Aidan's eyes narrowed as an intense sensation gripped him. The Demon Stone in his possession stirred, and Izen'draazt's malevolent influence washed over him. A dark compulsion drove him to the far end of the hall, where he found himself translating the twisted script of a hidden panel.

The others watched with bated breath as a doorway materialized, revealing a hidden passageway. Shadows curled like smoke, coalescing around him protectively.

"Izen'draazt wants me to follow," Aidan said, barely in control of his own voice.

Ahlissa exchanged a look with Jillian, both clearly troubled but resolved. "We'll be here if you need us."

The corridor opened into a dimly lit study, filled with arcane machinery and stacks of ancient scrolls. At the end of the room, a tall metal cabinet stood, its centre marked with a cavity that matched the shape of the Demon Stone perfectly. Izen'draazt's voice clawed at Aidan's mind, compelling him to place the stone inside. As the stone clicked into place, lights began to flicker within the cabinet, blinking in an ancient pattern of red, orange, and green.

The walls shimmered, and a dark portal spiralled open nearby, emitting a low hum that resonated with a sinister, otherworldly energy.

Aidan's blood ran cold as the shadowy form of Izen'draazt emerged from the portal. Towering over him, the demon's laughter filled his mind.

"You've served me well, mortal," Izen'draazt sneered, his voice echoing in Aidan's head. "Thanks to you, I am free once more."

Aidan felt his strength drain, his knees nearly buckling beneath the demon's overpowering presence. "Why use me? What do you want with this world?" he demanded, his voice trembling.

Izen'draazt's dark gaze settled on him. "A world to conquer, mortals to enslave. And you, my loyal instrument, will be spared. For now."

The demon's form faded, consumed by the swirling energy of the portal, which collapsed in a burst of blinding light. When Aidan's vision cleared, he was alone in the study, the apparatus powered down and silent.

He staggered back to the others, who looked at him in shock. "Izen'draazt... he's gone, but not forever. I couldn't stop him."

Ahlissa placed a hand on his shoulder, her expression sombre but determined. "We knew the risks. But he didn't escape through this world; he returned to The Eternal Void. That buys us time."

Aidan's heart was heavy with guilt, but he nodded. "It seems our journey here has only begun."

Outside the study, one of the scholars approached, holding an ancient metal box. "We found this in another chamber," he reported. "It contains manuscripts that may shed light on what truly happened here."

Aidan felt a flicker of hope. "Then let's take these back to the Zephyr Breeze. Perhaps the past has more secrets yet to reveal, and maybe, just maybe, we'll find a way to counter the threat Izen'draazt poses to our world."

16

The Path Back

Mysteries layered around Aidan as he mulled over the weight of the discoveries, they'd made during their perilous journey back from Qualtesh. Four days of gruelling travel through treacherous caverns led them back to the Zephyr Breeze, which, against all odds, lay untouched and undetected. As preparations for departure began, Aidan became absorbed in deciphering the ancient Kale Ashtari manuscripts they had unearthed. His attention wavered, though, as strange symbols on his deviant Aethyr Mark tingled, hinting at secrets yet untold.

The manuscripts revealed a grim history that set his mind spinning. The Kale Ashtari, once the proud, emotionless Khestar, had thrived on Scylla after their arrival on massive vessels that traversed the Void. Qualtesh had been their sanctuary, constructed on what they called a Power Node; a place of immense elemental and spiritual force. The city had flourished until a cataclysm shattered it, plunging the survivors into the earth where they grappled with the realization that no rescue would come. Trapped, they discovered that demonic entities, including one named Izen'draazt, guarded their prison beneath the surface.

Aidan shared the story with the scholars and mages on board, who were transfixed by the grim details of Qualtesh's descent into darkness. He was struck by one chilling line: *"The Demon Stone was crafted in secret, bound to hold Izen'draazt until a true descendant of the Kale Ashtari freed him, but only in their time."* How had he experienced Qualtesh as it was in the past? What had Izen'draazt done to him, manipulating him across time itself?

Word of these findings soon reached Athovhar, the esteemed representative of the Kale Ereshkigal, who summoned Aidan to discuss them.

Athovhar listened thoughtfully as Aidan recounted his journey, a flicker of intrigue on his otherwise composed face. "So Izen'draazt orchestrated events to find a Kale Ashtari descendant in the future," Athovhar surmised. "He sought someone who could wield the Demon Stone to release him into his past. Through you, he broke his bonds, stepping through the Void into our world. A demon's power to reach across time is not to be underestimated."

"But how is it possible?" Aidan asked, his voice hushed. "How could he remember me, prepare to find me in Kanarzand, and manipulate me into freeing him?"

Athovhar nodded. "Think of it as a cycle; a wheel within a wheel. When you freed him, he entered the past with a knowledge of you, creating a bond that led him to Kanarzand. Your actions are interconnected across time." He paused, his eyes gleaming with wisdom. "It's small consolation, perhaps, that he has retreated back to the Void. For now, your world remains unchanged."

Exiting Athovhar's quarters, Aidan felt the weight of his actions. Had he truly released Izen'draazt into the past? Was he responsible for the suffering that followed? Dark thoughts clouded his mind as the Zephyr Breeze ascended from the caverns, its path winding through the treacherous Labyrinth.

They emerged into the open plains, only to face a sudden, sand-swept storm on the horizon. Out of the churning dust, three skeletal airships emerged, emanating an ominous red glow and bristling with weaponry. Alqabda warships, armed with massive ballistae and jagged grapples. Panic spread among the crew as alarm bells rang, and Ahlissa's voice carried over the cacophony.

"All hands to battle stations! Ready the cannons!" she commanded, her face grim.

The enemy vessels closed in, preparing to unleash their assault when a crew member cried out, pointing through the storm. "Another vessel approaches! Something massive!"

A bolt of brilliant blue energy sliced through the storm, obliterating one of the Alqabda ships. Moments later, flashes of light scythed through the enemy formation, leaving one ship in ruins and the other limping away in retreat. As the storm abated, the crew gasped, staring at the massive shimmering airship that now hovered silently over the Zephyr Breeze. Its metallic hull gleamed with an otherworldly brilliance, and a low hum filled the air.

Ahlissa's hand rested on her sword as she scanned the craft. "The Stormbringer," she whispered, her voice filled with awe. "The legendary vessel. I had heard tales, but never believed them."

Jillian stepped forward, her eyes wide. "Is this...? But who controls it?"

"We're about to find out," Ahlissa replied, her tone cautious. A brilliant beam of light descended from the ship, washing over the deck and the crew without causing harm. "Stand down weapons, lower the shields!" she ordered, her voice steady. "Let's see what they want."

Aidan's breath caught as he felt a surge of energy pulse from the ship, and a moment later, his vision flooded with white light. He blinked, disoriented, to find himself alone in a small, smooth-walled room.

* * *

He took a step off the raised platform beneath him, his eyes adjusting to the clinical whiteness of his surroundings. Was this the inside of the Stormbringer? Unease settled over him as he realised he was separated from his crew. After a few minutes, the faint hum of approaching footsteps sounded beyond the wall, and with a hiss, the door slid open.

In the doorway stood a slender figure; a construct, not human, with an oval-shaped head and a smooth, featureless mask. Aidan took a tentative step forward and spoke, trying several languages, but the figure remained silent. It raised a slender arm, and from a small rod at its wrist, fired a white beam of light that struck Aidan's chest, leaving him unconscious.

When he awoke, he was restrained on a metallic table in another sterile room, his vision swimming from the lingering effects of the stun beam. Standing over him was a pale man, his white skin and long, golden hair pulled back in a top knot. His robes were finely embroidered, and his eyes held a cruel glint as he regarded Aidan.

The man spoke in a language that sounded like Aystaran but with unfamiliar inflections. Aidan strained to make sense of the words, catching only fragments until the man finally switched to a language he understood.

"You are different," the man said, studying Aidan with a mixture of curiosity and disdain. "You carry their signature in your blood, yet you are of this world. You are Aystaran?"

Aidan shook his head slightly. "I am half-Aystaran, yes, but my lineage... it may be more complicated than that."

The man's eyes gleamed. "So we have tracked. You ventured to Qualtesh, a place of my people long lost. And yet, you bear the Taint, a corruption we once sought to understand. It clings to you like a disease. Do you know its origin?"

Aidan nodded, the memories of his journey weighing heavily. "I found evidence of your people - the Khestar - adopting this Taint to protect themselves. They believed it would help them understand the enemies they faced. I encountered it at Star Haunt and in Qualtesh, where the Kale Ashtari struggled to escape."

The man's expression shifted as he listened, his eyes narrowing. "You say the Khestar willingly tainted themselves?" he asked, his voice cold.

"They were desperate. At Qualtesh, the survivors embraced darkness to resist their captors, including Izen'draazt," Aidan replied. "They even crafted the Demon Stone to capture him, but only one of their bloodline could release him. And now... I fear he has escaped."

A flicker of surprise crossed the man's face. "The Demon Stone? Such power, contained in that relic..." He stepped closer, his gaze piercing. "I am Khoresh of the Khestar," he finally revealed, a subtle pride colouring his voice. "We are not mere mortals, as you are beginning to understand. The Taint, however; this is something we never desired."

"So, you deny your people's choice?" Aidan's tone sharpened, a spark of defiance flaring within him. "The Taint gave the Khestar strength, even if it changed them."

Khoresh's gaze turned icy. "Strength or ruin? I know only that they sealed their own doom. Yet here you stand, carrying their corruption like a trophy. It is pathetic."

Aidan felt anger simmering beneath the surface, but he held his tongue. He was shackled, vulnerable, and facing an enemy far beyond his comprehension. For now, he needed answers more than he needed pride.

"What are you doing on this ship?" he finally asked. "Who controls the Stormbringer?"

Khoresh's lip curled into a slight smile. "The Stormbringer is a vessel of my people's design, a guardian of Scylla's remnants. You think you control your world, but it is we who shape your destiny. You have seen the Void between worlds; you know nothing of its true power."

"So, why bring me here?" Aidan asked, trying to keep his tone calm. "If I am as insignificant as you believe, why waste time on me?"

Khoresh studied him, considering the question. "Because you carry a piece of our history within you; a deviant Aethyr Mark tied to the Kale Ashtari. You have walked paths we had long thought lost, and perhaps, unknowingly, you are destined to open new ones."

The mention of his Aethyr Mark sent a shiver down Aidan's spine. He knew its sinister purpose, its link to Izen'draazt and the darkness lurking within him. But to hear that it held meaning even for the Khestar unsettled him deeply.

"So you seek to use me as a tool?" he asked, his voice barely more than a whisper.

Khoresh tilted his head, a mocking smile playing on his lips. "Perhaps. But tools are only useful if they survive the forge. Your journey has just begun, Aidan of Scylla. The Taint may yet reveal secrets you can't imagine." With that, Khoresh turned to the constructs and issued a curt command, and Aidan's restraints fell away.

Aidan rose slowly, rubbing his wrists, his gaze locked on Khoresh. "And where will this journey take me?"

Khoresh gestured toward the doorway. "That depends on how far you are willing to go. There are layers to our world, Aidan. Depths you've only begun to scratch. But if you are wise, you will leave here knowing that knowledge is not the same as power. Tread carefully."

17

Stormbringer

The metallic coldness of Khoresh's words jolted Aidan into focus. "*I am Khoresh of the Khestar.*" The proclamation resonated deeply, an echo from ancient texts where the Khestar were known as the Progenitors; the first to emerge from the darkness and tame Scylla's chaotic wilds. Aidan remembered studying these points of light, beacons of civilisation seeded by the Progenitors, as he'd seen inscribed in the ruins of Qualtesh. His thoughts faltered as Khoresh raised an eyebrow.

"Is something wrong?" Khoresh asked, a faint understanding flickering in his gaze. "All this must seem quite new to you."

"No, it's... I've read about the Progenitors, about those places of light you left behind," Aidan replied, the words feeling strange on his tongue. "The writings in Qualtesh echo that. They spoke of losing their path back to that light."

A thin smile passed over Khoresh's face. "Then you know of us," he replied. "Good." He gestured, and Aidan's restraints released. "Come.

I will take you to your friends, and we will share what hospitality we can."

A door slid open, revealing a corridor washed in stark white light. Khoresh strode ahead, leading Aidan to a spacious dining hall where Ahlissa, Jillian, and a handful of Khestar officers were eating in near silence. Ahlissa's eyes met his across the table, her expression a mix of guarded relief and curiosity. He took the seat offered and accepted a warm bowl of broth from a sleek metal assistant. The other Khestar officers, tall and stern, barely acknowledged their guests, continuing to eat without so much as a glance at their arrival.

"What do you make of this?" Jillian leaned in, keeping her voice low. "Are we prisoners?"

"I don't think so," Ahlissa replied thoughtfully. "They haven't treated us like prisoners. And considering they saved the Zephyr Breeze from an Alqabda ambush, I believe we're guests; though clearly under close observation." She turned to Aidan. "What did your host tell you?"

"He confirmed they're Khestar," Aidan said. "The original inhabitants of Scylla. They're the same people we've been searching for since Qualtesh."

Ahlissa's eyes widened in surprise. "The Progenitors? Really?" She seemed to consider this, glancing around at the advanced metalwork and quiet efficiency of their hosts. "It would explain the technology. We use a fraction of their methods in our own airships, integrated from what we thought were myths."

Jillian, overhearing, nodded. "I told them I was Khystar, and they seemed familiar with my people's struggles. They mentioned the Sah'ren and said my homeland is not the only place where such threats exist. Strangely, I feel at ease here, as though I've found something that calls to me."

"Yes," Ahlissa replied softly, "as do I. They have an air of calm authority, not unlike our own people." She smiled at Aidan. "So, did they figure out what you are?"

"Not exactly," Aidan admitted, "but they did conclude that I'm neither entirely Kale Khestari nor Adeni. I think they're as curious as we are."

Dinner continued in a steady rhythm, each course rich with spices and flavours foreign to Aidan's senses but filling. After a time, Khoresh approached with an invitation to relax in a nearby lounge. Soft seating and cushioned couches were arranged in the room, and small trays of mulled wine waited for them. As they settled in, Aidan noticed a panel on the wall flicker to life, displaying images and scenes. Some of the Khestar watched the screen intently, and Khoresh noted Aidan's curiosity.

"A device for our amusement," he explained, offering a rare smile. "It plays information as well as entertainment. An indulgence, perhaps."

Aidan nodded, filing away the knowledge, his thoughts swirling around the contradictions of the Khestar; so close to his own people, yet so vastly different. His observations were cut short as Khoresh invited them on a tour of the ship.

They moved through hallways filled with humming consoles, past control stations, engineering decks, and sleek quarters, each step revealing more advanced and mystifying equipment. Khoresh provided descriptions that sometimes felt like riddles, explaining concepts beyond Aidan's understanding; dimensional gates, ionized particles, planar shields. Ahlissa drank in the explanations with rapt attention, her questions stretching Khoresh's descriptions as he struggled to simplify the terms.

Their host gestured to the shimmering walls, explaining that the ship, known as Void Ship 22 of the Third Battle Group, traversed distant realms using dimensional shifts. Though his words were often incomprehensible, Aidan pieced together enough to sense its uniqueness. "But perhaps you know it best by the name given in your world - Stormbringer," Khoresh added with a wry smile.

The term made Ahlissa raise her eyebrows. "Stormbringer. So, you've truly been watching Scylla all this time?"

Khoresh inclined his head. "Yes. We maintain watch, particularly over ancient installations like Platform One. Your world, Scylla, contains many points of interest to us."

"Platform One?" Aidan asked, recalling the ruin near Qualtesh.

"An ancient facility, one of many," Khoresh explained. "Built to anchor certain energies in your world. It was disrupted recently; a disturbance which drew us here. Your Zephyr Breeze merely provided an opportunity to aid you while observing."

"Why does the platform matter?" Ahlissa asked.

"Imagine a world plagued by chaos, by things that defy the natural order," Khoresh replied. "We - our people - seek stability, so we created these platforms to maintain order across worlds."

Aidan was about to ask another question when the mention of Izen'draazt brought him to silence. The demon's name chilled the air as Khoresh elaborated.

"Izen'draazt remains in the Void, drifting within the remnants of the dark fragment that fell upon Kanarzand. His power is fractured, but we keep vigil. For now, he waits."

Aidan felt a pang of dread as Khoresh continued. "He's linked to you, Aidan. That link alerted us to your presence. You may know him well, yes?"

Aidan swallowed. "Yes. In Qualtesh, I released him; or rather, in his past." He recounted the twisted reality he had faced, the feeling of being manipulated through time.

Khoresh raised a hand, listening in silent understanding. "Time flows strangely around certain beings. It's entirely possible that Izen'draazt manipulated you, waiting patiently across ages. His patience is legendary."

"I've seen what he left behind in Qualtesh and the Star Haunt," Aidan said, his voice quiet. "I've seen the symbol he left; the one that now marks my skin."

Khoresh's eyes gleamed as he took in Aidan's words. "You bear a deviant Aethyr Mark? Show me."

Aidan rolled back his sleeve to reveal the serpentine symbol etched into his skin, a dark reminder of his journey. Khoresh examined it, his face carefully controlled.

"This symbol hasn't been seen in eons," he remarked. "It belonged to rebellious factions among the Khestar who sought power beyond what we allowed. The Sceptre Guilds in your world would likely seek to erase you for bearing it."

Aidan studied Khoresh's expression, half expecting condemnation. "I don't know why I bear it. It's something I don't fully understand."

Khoresh's gaze softened. "You carry the blood of those who survived Qualtesh. That mark ties you to both Scylla and the Khestar. And so, despite the shadows it carries, it makes you one of us."

Ahlissa and Jillian exchanged glances, visibly taken aback. Aidan felt a strange weight lift as Khoresh acknowledged his lineage; a hesitant but profound connection he hadn't expected.

"No one should see the Kale Ashtari as fallen," Aidan finally said. "They fought for survival the only way they knew, even embracing darkness to resist."

Khoresh nodded solemnly. "We shall remember them as heroes; the lost people who clung to the light as long as they could."

With the tour nearing its end, Khoresh presented each of them with an oblong, crystal-infused device. "This will allow you to communicate with us," he explained, holding one out to Aidan. "In times of dire need, speak my name. If we are within range, we shall respond. You are kin."

They returned to a small chamber with a raised platform, identical to the one where Aidan had first awakened. Khoresh assured them that this device would transport them to the deck of the Zephyr Breeze. "When you're on board, signal us. We will create a portal to bring you back to Gideon in mere hours. Consider it a gift for the knowledge you have given us."

As the platform hummed, Ahlissa inclined her head. "Thank you, Khoresh. We will remember this encounter and honour the memory of those we discussed."

With a flash, they appeared on the deck of the Zephyr Breeze, the familiar sight of the airship's decor reassuring them. True to his word, Khoresh's vessel materialized nearby, creating a portal that roiled the sky with storms as it engulfed the airship, hurling them across the skies of Scylla. In mere moments, they saw the coast of Gideon rising ahead.

After so long, the gleaming spires and bustling city were a welcome sight. Aidan looked at Jillian. "There'll be questions waiting for us in Gideon City, given how we left."

Jillian chuckled. "I hope they're ready for the answers."

18

Gideon City

Upon landing at the outskirts of Gideon, Aidan sensed an immediate shift in the atmosphere. The airship port, now bathed in the early evening glow, was abuzz with an unusual sight: a new militia force, scanning each disembarking crew member with wary eyes.

"Who do these militia answer to?" Ahlissa demanded, watching as a uniformed officer meticulously recorded their identities.

"The Sentinel," a guard replied. "They were instated by The Thirteen, upon the Sceptre Guilds' recommendation. The Fixer oversaw negotiations to ensure the city's security was sound."

A chill ran through Aidan. The Observers were known for tracking down those with deviant Aethyr Marks. His hand drifted toward the mark concealed beneath his sleeve, the one that tied him to Izen'draazt. Ahlissa's words cut through his thoughts.

"We're aware of the risks, Aidan. Blend in, keep calm, and follow my lead." She leaned closer. "Tonight, we dine with the Aystar Ambassador at the Liberty Spire. Let's relax, regroup, and keep up appearances."

Aidan nodded, still tense. "Jillian should come too. But... in disguise."

"Indeed," Ahlissa replied. "She knows the risks. Invite her, and we'll depart in two hours."

When Aidan approached Jillian, she welcomed the invitation with a grin. "I'll come as Coralee Shyvath tonight. A look that's exotic but practical. Meet you on deck."

The militia, eyes sharp, barely nodded as Aidan, Jillian- now a mysterious woman draped in dark silks - and Ahlissa presented the ambassador's invitation and passed through. The streets of Gideon felt different: quieter, with fewer Argar in sight. Even those who appeared had bundled themselves heavily, concealing their faces. The driver of their sail barge noticed Aidan's gaze lingering on the changed cityscape.

"Don't worry too much about the militia, sir," the driver commented, keeping his voice low. "People say they're looking for monsters."

Aidan's eyes narrowed, noting the Argar's discomfort. "An occupation, but a peaceful one, for now," he murmured to Ahlissa.

She nodded. "Yet, what lies beneath the surface is what matters."

Inside the Liberty Spire, they were ushered to a table with a commanding view of the dining hall. Bright lights and laughter masked the tension simmering below the surface. Aidan scanned the room cautiously, noting familiar faces; Master Brevax, Mhorvaeus, and two council members, the Adjudicator and the Gatherer, seated nearby.

However, three men in white shirts and broad-brimmed hats stood out, their dark eyes fixed on the crowd. Observers.

Aidan pointed them out to Ahlissa and Jillian. "The Observers. They're watching us, or at least watching for us."

Jillian's eyes flickered toward them. "They're just like the ones we saw at the inn, right before we set off on this journey. They didn't come to eat; they came to observe."

At that moment, Ambassador Aren Shivaleth approached, his warm smile contrasting with the intensity of the evening. "Ahlissa, Aidan, Jillian - what a pleasure. I've been eager to hear about your journey." He leaned closer, lowering his voice. "Especially the shard. And the tales Athovhar brought back about you, Aidan. He said you represent the best of us; Khestari courage tempered by remarkable restraint. He has quite a high opinion of you."

Aidan inclined his head. "The Kale Ashtari's story deserves to be told, Ambassador, but not with sadness. They fought for survival and were driven by necessity, not evil."

As the ambassador absorbed his words, Aidan caught Mhorvaeus watching from across the hall. The man's gaze was unmistakable, his presence reinforced by the small entourage surrounding him. When their eyes met, Mhorvaeus's thin smile was less a greeting than a taunt.

"Mhorvaeus is paying close attention," Aidan murmured to Ahlissa.

"Let him," she replied with a smirk. "He sent his minions to chase us across kingdoms without success."

As they spoke, Ahlissa's betrothed, Ivistar Immiar, approached her, prompting her to excuse herself from the table. She returned an hour later with news.

"The Kale Khestari are restless. They're deploying resources to northern outposts. Reports of Sindarr incursions, likely by Sceptre Guild mercenaries and Mhargrave academics, have stirred resentment. Ivistar himself has been ordered to oversee the situation."

Aidan nodded. "There must be something the Sceptre Guilds are after. They wouldn't risk this otherwise."

Ahlissa's face darkened. "Precisely. Such trespasses on sacred land could lead to war. My people are volatile. If the intrusions continue, they won't hold back."

Their conversation shifted as Ahlissa voiced her concerns about Jillian. "Jillian's return to Gideon puts her in grave danger. The Aldrosian Zealot agents hunt her, and their influence in this city is growing. I worry about her safety. Perhaps you could persuade her to join the Khestar?"

Aidan considered, glancing at Jillian as she approached the table. "I agree. But I also think we should address the agents here. A discreet but decisive move might keep them off her trail. However, stirring up conflict would only justify further militia presence."

Ahlissa's eyes gleamed. "So, we focus on Sindarr's incursions and cut off outside interference at its source?"

Aidan nodded. "Exactly. If we eliminate the external threat, we can contain the internal situation here."

Ahlissa's lips curved in a pleased smile. "Ivistar would appreciate your support. It may even earn you his respect. This plan could stabilize tensions here while preserving our heritage."

Just then, Jillian leaned in. "Is everything alright? You two look serious. And did you notice the Observers? They're unsettling."

Aidan nodded. "Yes, and your presence here may have attracted the agents you've evaded. They're in the city, at least five of them. I fear you're in more danger than ever."

Jillian's face hardened. "If that's true, they'll have to be dealt with. My people may be peaceful, but we defend ourselves. These agents aren't even human any more. They're vessels for entities from another realm, and they must be stopped."

Aidan lowered his voice. "We could use a controlled environment outside the city to lure them in. If you're willing, we could set a trap."

Jillian's eyes lit with determination. "Where?"

Aidan thought for a moment. "The ancient ruins we explored, near the Sun Tower and King Thalendir's tomb, with its labyrinthine tunnels. They're perfect for an ambush."

Ahlissa's face brightened. "That could work. We could coordinate with my forces to handle the situation quietly."

As their strategy began to take shape, the ambassador, who had taken to the dance floor, returned to the table. "Everything satisfactory? It's a pleasant change from our usual struggles - no fighting, no political tension."

Aidan nodded, forcing a polite smile. "The evening has been wonderful, Ambassador."

During the lull in conversation, Aidan caught sight of Master Brevax and approached him. The older man looked worn and frail, yet his smile was warm as they greeted each other.

"Aidan, my boy... back at last." He studied Aidan with tired eyes. "Did you find the knowledge you sought?"

"Yes, Master. I've written an account of my experiences, as I promised. It includes my journey to Kanarzand and an encounter with the great library at Cordovar."

Master Brevax accepted the scroll with a fond smile, examining it with reverence. "You've always been a remarkable scholar. That's why I took you on as my apprentice. We've had some grand adventures, haven't we?"

Aidan smiled. "Thank you for everything, Master. I owe my skills to your guidance. But tell me, how are things here in Gideon?"

Master Brevax's expression turned sombre. "The city grows more restrictive each day. The Mhargraves have implemented severe restrictions on historical study. It's eerily reminiscent of Kanarzand's final days."

Aidan's voice dropped. "I have contacts at the Cordovar Library who could publish your work discreetly. The truth about Kanarzand must be known, to prevent Gideon from repeating its mistakes."

Master Brevax's eyes gleamed with hope. "You're right. The story must be told. Perhaps we can still make a difference."

"Yes, I've noticed the changes myself," Aidan continued. "The militia presence, the quiet streets; Argar are scarce, and the market feels subdued."

"Yes, change is sweeping over Gideon, for better or worse. I long to return to the desert, to rebuild the library we lost in Kanarzand."

Aidan placed a hand on his mentor's shoulder. "Build it here, quietly. If the ruling forces are brought down, you'll have a repository of truth ready."

The old man's eyes glistened. "You give me hope, Aidan. I will take your advice and start again."

They parted with a quiet understanding, both aware of the mounting risks. Aidan watched his mentor leave, then turned back to the table, feeling the weight of responsibility settle over him.

* * *

The next morning, Aidan, Jillian, and Ahlissa met privately to solidify their plan. They would draw the agents out, luring them to the Sun Tower ruins. The Zephyr Breeze would serve as both a decoy and a safe exit, ensuring that the encounter would remain concealed from the city's watchful eye.

With their preparations set, Aidan felt a strange mixture of excitement and trepidation. The upcoming ambush would serve as both a resolution and a warning, a message to those who sought to control and suppress. The past they were uncovering, the stories lost to time, belonged not to rulers or councils, but to everyone.

19

The Kale Ashtari Manuscripts

As Aidan settled into the quiet corner of the Zephyr Breeze's study room, he carefully unrolled the manuscripts one by one, his curiosity sharpened by the tantalizing clues they offered into the lost history of the Khestar and their descendants, the Kale Ashtari. A thick layer of dust and age clung to each brittle sheet, but the contents, written in the ancient, flowing script, held an undeniable vitality, transporting him to another time, another world.

The first scroll he opened held a mesmerizing account of life on the home world of the Khestar. Aidan read of a vibrant, advanced society that spanned across realms, spreading "points of light" wherever they travelled. These outposts - strategically chosen across worlds in the multiverse - served as bastions against an ever-encroaching darkness that, they believed, sought to quench the light. It described the Khestar's vigilance, their sense of duty to uphold civilisation against the forces of chaos and evil. Aidan traced his fingers along the lines, feeling as though he could almost see the Khestar warriors and scholars rallying to defend these beacons of hope. Yet, the Khestar also understood the cost of vigilance, as these journeys often meant long separations from home and loved ones.

Aidan leaned back, imagining this noble race standing watch over realms, poised to confront the shadows. It was a grimly fitting parallel to his own mission.

Turning to another manuscript, Aidan discovered a detailed account of Kale Ashtari art and culture. The pages were filled with descriptions of vibrant murals that adorned their underground city of Qualtesh. He was surprised to find that the artwork's themes ranged from battle scenes to moments of family and community celebration. The manuscript described how colour itself was of tremendous importance to the Kale Ashtari, reflecting their state of mind. Even in the darkness, they sought light, painting luminous murals with crushed crystals that glowed in the dim caverns. The art forms they developed were born from their harsh reality; reflections of beauty that thrived despite the absence of sunlight. Aidan could almost envision the stark reds, deep purples, and glistening whites against the rough stone walls, offering a fleeting beauty in the cold underground halls.

One manuscript provided a delightful contrast to the others: it detailed a variety of puzzles and games popular among the Kale Ashtari. Aidan chuckled at the thought of these games serving as a rare reprieve for a people burdened by survival and the constant looming presence of darkness. The puzzles were complex, often based on layered logic and intricate symbolism. One puzzle detailed in the manuscript required arranging symbols representing the elements of light and shadow into a harmonious balance. He couldn't help but feel intrigued, wondering if he could solve these ancient games himself. The games must have offered not only distraction but also a mental exercise, sharpening the wits of players against the very concepts they fought against in real life.

Aidan's gaze shifted to a large, dense tome, and as he opened it, he was greeted by a section on cooking. Recipes, each meticulously detailed, listed ingredients and measurements, though he found himself chuckling at some unfamiliar items such as "essence of crystalflower." He imagined the Kale Ashtari cooks bustling in their kitchens, experimenting with these ingredients, creating dishes that perhaps held some faint, comforting echo of the home world they'd lost. The recipes weren't just for sustenance; they seemed intended to uplift, to offer comfort to those confined in eternal darkness. He lingered over a recipe for spiced broth made from rare underground herbs, a staple meal for warriors preparing for battle, or families gathering for an evening meal.

The next scroll was different. It presented a philosophical debate on the nature of intelligence and existence, exploring what it meant to be a creature of will, wisdom, and intellect. Part metaphysical and part spiritual, the manuscript ventured into the realms of law versus chaos, good versus evil, presenting them as cosmic forces in an eternal struggle. The idea of neutrality between these extremes captivated Aidan, who saw reflections of his own inner conflicts mirrored in the text. The manuscript argued that only by embracing a balance could one truly wield their wisdom with understanding. He marvelled at the manuscript's introspection, wondering if the Kale Ashtari wrote it as a way to understand their own descent into darkness.

A sudden chill passed over him as he reached the next manuscript. The dark, almost oppressive aura of the pages was unmistakable. Here were tomes devoted to the worship of Izen'draazt, the dark demon who had ensnared the Kale Ashtari, marking a shift in their history - a painful fracture where they ceased to be Khestar and became something else. Aidan read how the people of Qualtesh, trapped beneath the ground, had finally surrendered to despair, accepting their new fate under Izen'draazt's dominion. With their hearts embittered and minds twisted by Dark Aethyr, they forsook their identity, cutting ties with their Khestar heritage. The writing was fevered, desperate, and Aidan felt the weight of their anguish and hopelessness, a people who, isolated and besieged by demonic entities, had turned to the very darkness they once fought.

Two manuscripts on shadow magic and the dark arts followed, and Aidan forced himself to delve into their pages, despite his unease. The knowledge within was powerful but tainted, filled with spells and rituals that manipulated shadow and tapped into energies that felt cold and foreign to him. Yet, he could see why the Kale Ashtari, cut off from light, would cling to shadow magic as their only means of defence, their only way to maintain control. This power, though twisted, was all they had in the endless darkness.

Aidan paused before opening the final manuscript, a strange thrill tingling his fingers. This one described the nine platforms that the Khestar had established on Scylla. There was no map, but the descriptions were clear, marking each platform by nearby landmarks, creatures, and the specific environmental conditions surrounding them. Aidan read eagerly, his mind whirring with connections and possibilities. The platforms were likely remnants of the Khestar's original colonization mission, and they might contain powerful relics or technology. His eyes sparkled as he realised that this was more than just a list of ancient sites; it was a treasure map, a guide to the lost history of his world.

The words conjured vivid images in his mind; the rugged cliff side of one platform, guarded by serpentine creatures that breathed fire; another hidden within the dense mists of a jungle, accessible only through paths visible at twilight; and yet another located on a coastal plain where, according to the text, the tides revealed a hidden pathway. Each description beckoned, and he felt an urgent desire to set out on a journey to each one, to uncover the secrets they held.

He closed the manuscripts, leaning back with a satisfied sigh but also a growing sense of purpose. He had only begun to scratch the surface of the Khestar's legacy, a civilisation that had spanned realms and upheld points of light in a multiverse riddled with darkness. But there was so much more to learn, to uncover, to protect. These manuscripts were the beginning of a quest that would span worlds and ideals; a journey to preserve the knowledge and light of the past and to understand the darkness that had once nearly consumed it.

The silence around him seemed almost alive with expectation, as if the ancient authors themselves were watching, waiting to see what he would do with this newfound knowledge.

20

The Ambassador

The trio - Ahlissa, Jillian, and Aidan - followed the ambassador's servants through the corridors of the Aystaran Embassy, dimly lit with soft, blue-hued lanterns. Aren Shivaleth, the Aystaran ambassador, was a tall, austere figure known for his perceptive nature and measured authority. He led them to his private chambers where the heavy velvet curtains blocked out the glare of the midday sun. The chamber had a sense of tranquillity, a haven from the tension that roiled within Gideon's city walls.

The ambassador's piercing eyes fell upon each of them as he welcomed them and gestured for them to take a seat. "Tell me everything," he said simply, his tone a blend of curiosity and concern.

Over the next hour, Aidan, Ahlissa, and Jillian recounted the journey that had occupied them for the past seven months. From their initial discovery of Qualtesh's location to their journey through treacherous caverns and the strange encounters with shadow creatures, they described each moment, each peril, with a thoroughness that left no detail spared. They spoke of their alliance with the Khestar, their encounter with the ancient guardian at the Star Haunt, and Aidan's terrifying battle with the demonic presence of Izen'draazt.

When they had finally recounted everything, Shivaleth leaned back, his face solemn as he absorbed the weight of their words. He took a moment before responding, his gaze lingering thoughtfully on Aidan. "You have seen much of our history, long-lost to us," he said, his voice carrying a reverent note. "While we had hoped the shard would unlock secrets, I would argue that what you uncovered is far greater. It is clear now that we have allies in the Khestar, and we are safe in the knowledge that they guard our world from threats we may never fully understand."

His gaze fixed on Aidan, and he continued, "And you, Aidan, have gained insight into your lineage. Yours is a heritage more ancient than any of us had imagined, connecting you to a history of resilience and bravery. Among all our people, you are unique. You are not just Aystar; your blood carries the strength and purpose of the Khestar."

Aidan felt a mixture of pride and disbelief at the ambassador's words. He had always known his heritage was unusual, but this connection to the Khestar, the legendary Progenitors, gave him a newfound sense of purpose. However, Aren's tone shifted, his expression more sombre.

"There is more I must tell you," Aren said quietly. "We have recently discovered that some of the Kale Ashtari did escape the depths of Qualtesh. A small band of survivors made their way across the continent, eventually finding a life within the Argar Empire. They settled in the place we now call the Star Haunt, resuming their identity as Khestar." Aren's voice grew softer, laced with a gravity that made Aidan's heart pound. "Aidan, we believe that your mother was one of those Kale Ashtari."

Aidan's breath caught. He had always wondered about his mother's origins, the strange powers she had hinted at before her death. But Aren wasn't finished.

"It is likely your mother met your father in Sindarr," Aren explained. "And it is also possible she was killed by the Twelve, the Arcane Council from Kanarzand. They have long dictated which Aethyr Marks are permitted, and which are declared deviant. If your mother bore an aberrant Aethyr Mark, that would have been reason enough for the Twelve to silence her and your father."

Aidan felt an icy dread settle over him as Aren continued. He had never truly known what happened to his parents, but to hear it described so plainly, as murder, was jarring.

Aren placed a steadying hand on Aidan's shoulder. "I am sorry to share such tragic news, but I believe you deserved to know the truth. What you carry, Aidan, is their legacy – a legacy that the Twelve sought to erase."

Aidan clenched his jaw. The Twelve, with their arrogance and desire to control all magic, had unwittingly set him on this path. And here he was, their worst nightmare: a bearer of the very Aethyr Mark they had tried to wipe out.

Aren continued, "Athovhar, the Deathless representative from Kale Ereshkigal, spoke highly of you, Aidan. For one of his kind to recognise your heritage, and you as a bearer of that legacy, is a rare honour indeed."

Aidan's mind was a tempest of emotions. He felt pride, anger, and a sense of determination deep within him. This legacy was his to bear, and he would not allow it to be erased or hidden.

The conversation shifted to the current state of Gideon City, and Aidan voiced his concerns, wary of the changes he had sensed since their return. "The city seems different," he said. "The council is fostering a climate of fear, much like what led to the downfall of Kanarzand. It's as if the mistakes of the past are repeating."

Aren's expression darkened, and he nodded. "Gideon is not the safe haven it once was. The council, particularly the Thirteen, has grown erratic, less open to negotiation. Diplomacy is increasingly challenging. This new militia force on the streets seems to be backed by Sindarr and possibly by the Sceptre Guilds. There's a hardline shift, a sense that power is tightening."

Jillian, who had been listening intently, interjected. "And what of the Aldrosian mission? I have reason to believe that agents of the Aspiring Dream have infiltrated the council, their influence poisoning the city from within."

Aren's eyes flicked to her, weighing her words. "We have seen changes, yes, but proof is difficult to come by. Their influence is insidious, veiled behind allies and associates. Yet, I fear you may be right – the decisions of the council have grown increasingly ruthless."

Jillian's eyes narrowed with a steely resolve. "I have felt their presence. The Zealots are here, controlling the council through manipulation. We must stop them."

Ahlissa broke in, her tone calm but filled with a barely contained intensity. "Ambassador, that is precisely what we have been preparing for. We have a plan."

Aren's eyebrow rose, intrigued. "Please, tell me more."

Ahlissa leaned forward, speaking in hushed, determined tones. "Our plan hinges on using the council's overreach and hidden agendas to our advantage. We have noticed that while they fortify Gideon, there are unchecked incursions into Aystaran lands, particularly areas holding ancient ruins and artefacts. We intend to confront these encroachments and bring back evidence of what they're after. If we expose their hidden motives and tie them to foreign powers, it might rally enough support to curb their influence."

Aidan added, "These incursions are led by mercenaries and archaeologists associated with the Mhargrave Outreach Society, backed by Sceptre Guilds from Sindarr. The sites they've targeted are sacred to the Aystaran people. By protecting them, we're not only upholding Aystaran sovereignty, but we're also establishing a line in the sand that the council and their allies can't cross."

Aren nodded, an approving gleam in his eyes. "This plan has merit. If these intrusions into Aystaran lands can be documented and connected to Gideon's council, then their support may falter."

Jillian spoke up, her tone laced with determination. "There's also another matter – my own safety. With the increased presence of the Aldrosian Zealots in Gideon, I'm in constant danger here. Their agents are ruthless, and they will stop at nothing to silence me."

Aren's expression softened with understanding. "I can provide you with protection here at the embassy, but that won't be enough if the council becomes involved. If it's true that they're controlling the council's decisions, then you are at risk everywhere within the city walls."

Aidan took a deep breath, the solution forming in his mind. "What if we lured the Zealots out of Gideon? There's a place we discovered, an ancient ruin beyond the city's reach. We could set a trap there, where the council's eyes don't reach."

Ahlissa's eyes gleamed with approval. "That's exactly what we need. We can draw them out, expose them, and remove their influence one by one."

The ambassador looked at each of them in turn, considering the boldness of their plan. "If you are prepared for the risks, then I shall assist you in any way I can. I will support your efforts to preserve Aystaran sovereignty, and I will ensure that any discoveries we make are protected under diplomatic immunity."

Aidan felt a renewed sense of purpose. This plan, as dangerous as it was, would allow them to reclaim what was lost and restore the balance that Gideon's council sought to disrupt. They would honour the legacy of the Khestar and the Kale Ashtari, and they would stand united against the insidious darkness that had begun to worm its way into the city.

They spent the rest of the evening refining their strategy, mapping out the ancient ruins they would protect and the traps they would set for their enemies. The night stretched on, but their spirits were high. As they finally took their leave, Aidan felt a quiet sense of determination settle over him. The council and the Twelve had tried to erase his lineage, but they had failed. His mother's legacy would live on, and he would ensure that Gideon remembered the true heritage of the Aystaran people.

21

The Resupply Mission

Ahlissa's decision to spread word of the Zephyr Breeze's mission was a calculated risk, but she had taken every precaution to ensure their plan would draw the Aldrosian Zealots of The Aspiring Dream into their trap. The message was clear: supplies were being delivered to Aystaran outposts and archaeological sites in the southeastern desert, culminating in a stop at the ruins of the Sun Tower.

The ghostly citadel held grim significance for the Aystaran people. It was here that the Kale Khestari suffered their ultimate defeat against the Argar thousands of years ago, a battle that left the once-mighty settlers shattered. Now, the haunted ruins would serve a new purpose: an ambush for the Aldrosian agents who hunted Jillian.

As supplies were loaded onto the Zephyr Breeze, Ahlissa met with the Aystaran Ambassador, Aren Shivaleth, to brief him on their plans. The ambassador listened attentively, nodding in approval.

"A wise plan," he said. "This spares me the unpleasant task of explaining to the council why Aystar are engaged in open combat within

Gideon's streets." He leaned back, his expression thoughtful. "If you need further assistance -"

"We have everything covered," Ahlissa interrupted gently. "The Machination has ensured that contingencies are in place."

"Excellent," Shivaleth replied, his lips curling into a wry smile. "That gives me plausible deniability. If anyone questions the disappearance of these Zealots, I'll be none the wiser."

After a formal dinner that evening, the ambassador retired, leaving Aidan and the others to their quarters. The Zephyr Breeze was set to depart at first light.

By dawn, the airship was bustling with activity. The supplies were loaded, the crew made their final checks, and a small diplomatic escort ensured their departure went smoothly. Aidan stood on the deck, gazing out over the sprawling city of Gideon, its streets quieter than he remembered. The oppressive presence of the new militia loomed over the populace, and he felt a pang of unease as he thought of what the city might become.

Ahlissa moved to the bridge to oversee preparations, while Aidan and Jillian headed to their quarters. The tension in the air was palpable. As they entered, Jillian paused, her eyes narrowing as though she could sense something unseen.

"Aidan," she said softly, "I need to talk to you."

He nodded, ushering her inside. "Of course. What's on your mind?"

Jillian sat down, her expression serious. "I can feel them. The Zealots. They're watching me."

"How do you know? Is it through magic?" he asked.

"No," she replied. "It's something deeper. We Khystar can tune into vibrations, a telepathic resonance that allows us to sense intent. They've locked onto me. I know they'll follow us once we leave Gideon."

Aidan frowned. "That's exactly what we want, but are you ready for this?"

Jillian gave a small nod, though her brow furrowed. "I've been meditating on The Path of Light. I'm preparing myself mentally and spiritually to face them. But I needed you to know that the plan is working. They will come."

Aidan placed a reassuring hand on her shoulder. "You're not alone in this. If you need anything - anything at all - just ask. I'll stand beside you."

Jillian smiled faintly. "Thank you. Your support means more than you know." She rose and left to continue her meditation.

The Zephyr Breeze soared over the arid expanse of the southeastern desert, its engines humming steadily. Over the next four days, they made several stops at Aystaran war clan outposts and archaeological sites, delivering much-needed supplies.

At each stop, Aidan observed the state of the Aystaran encampments. The war clans were well-organized, their warriors standing tall and vigilant. At one remote outpost, he watched as children peeked out from behind their parents, their bright eyes filled with curiosity and a hint of fear at the sight of the massive airship. Aidan handed out small tokens - coins, beads, and charms - to ease their anxiety, earning shy smiles in return.

The archaeological sites were equally fascinating. A small shrine in one location bore inscriptions that Aidan recognised as ancient Khestar script, though much of it was eroded. At another stop, a circle of standing stones radiated faint magical energy, a testament to its enduring connection to the Aethyr. Aidan spent an hour at each site, recording notes and deciphering fragments, his scholarly instincts keeping him focused even as his mind lingered on the impending confrontation.

As the Zephyr Breeze drew closer to the ruins of the Sun Tower, Ahlissa called a meeting with Aidan and Jillian in her quarters. A large map of the citadel ruins lay unfurled on the table, its surface marked with strategic annotations.

"This is where we'll lead them," Ahlissa said, pointing to the citadel's location on a map. "It's isolated and defensible. The ruins provide plenty of cover for our forces, and the surrounding desert will make it difficult for the Zealots to retreat."

Aidan studied the map. "The ruins are steeped in shadow magic. It's likely the Zealots will feel empowered there. We'll need to be cautious."

Jillian nodded. "They'll underestimate us, thinking they have the upper hand. That's where we'll strike."

Ahlissa's eyes gleamed with determination. "We'll position our forces here and here," she said, indicating choke points around the ruins. "Aidan, you and Jillian will draw them in. Once they're committed, we'll close the trap."

Aidan clenched his fists, feeling the weight of responsibility. "Understood. Let's make sure this ends here."

22

The Ruined Citadel

The ruins of the Sun Tower had undergone a transformation since Aidan had last seen it. Once shrouded beneath shifting desert sands, the fortress now stood as a testament to the power of Sand Magic, an ancient and specialized discipline that had thrived in Kanarzand. Aidan had never studied this magic himself, but its influence was undeniable: towering battlements, stone walls, and soaring towers were revealed in their full grandeur. The excavated citadel had returned to life as an imposing stronghold, watched over by an entire war clan of Kale Khestari warriors.

Commander Skaros Tyrellen greeted them warmly as they disembarked from the Zephyr Breeze. He exuded strength and confidence, his sharp eyes and polished armour a reflection of the disciplined warriors under his command. His demeanour softened as he addressed Aidan.

"I've heard much of you, Aidan," Skaros began. "Your former tutor, Lorian Tyraleth, speaks highly of you, often recounting your skill with the blade and your quick learning as a ranger. His son, Tiralas, owes you his life for saving him from the Zar'tul ambush at Athosin. Among our people, you are regarded not just as a scholar but as a hero. You are worthy of being called brother."

Aidan blinked in surprise. The praise was unexpected, but he inclined his head respectfully. "That means a great deal to me. Thank you."

Ahlissa grinned at the exchange, clearly pleased. Jillian, standing slightly apart, looked impressed.

"We bring news," Ahlissa said, shifting the conversation to business. "And more importantly, we bring much-needed supplies."

Skaros turned to his warriors, barking a quick command. The Kale Khestari moved with practiced efficiency, unloading the ship under the commander's watchful eye. "What is the news you bring?" he asked, turning back to Ahlissa.

Her tone grew sombre. "Gideon grows darker. Corruption festers within the city, spreading fear and mistrust among its people. The Thirteen are fractured, and we suspect Sindarr's influence is at the heart of the unrest. Worse, scholars are now forbidden from studying this region's history. Where Izen'draazt failed to extinguish Gideon's light, something else may be succeeding."

Skaros frowned. "This is troubling. We will remain vigilant. While we have no desire to fight Gideon's people, we will defend our own if they bring harm to us."

"It may not come to that," Ahlissa reassured him. "The Ambassador and our allies are working to uncover the cause. With luck, the situation can be reversed - or at least contained."

Skaros nodded but didn't look convinced. "Corruption spreads like a poison. Sometimes it's necessary to cut off a limb to save the body."

Aidan smirked, appreciating the commander's pragmatism. "I couldn't agree more."

Skaros led them through the central keep, showing them to their quarters on the second floor. The rooms were modest but functional, each offering privacy and a place to wash away the dust of the journey. After allowing them time to settle in, Skaros returned, a rare smile lighting his stern features.

"This place has changed since your last visit," he said, laughing lightly. "I know that's an understatement, but I think you'll find this tour quite illuminating."

They followed him through the fortress. The battlements provided a commanding view of the desert, where the rippling sands stretched endlessly to the horizon. From the towers, Skaros pointed out features newly uncovered by the excavation efforts: a well surrounded by crumbled walls, likely the citadel's original water source, the remains of a buried sail barge, its sleek lines strangely reminiscent of airships, and a temple thought to be dedicated to ancestor worship, its design reflecting Aystaran craftsmanship.

The desert breeze whispered through the ruins as the group paused to take in the sights.

"It has changed indeed, and for the better," Aidan said.

"Yes," Skaros agreed. "This place is sacred to us. For the Aystar, it

163

represents shame in their defeat. But for the Kale Khestari, it's a symbol of resilience. It was here that we fought to the last, proving our strength and resolve. Reclaiming this citadel is a statement to any who would challenge us: this land is ours."

"It is also a reminder of hope," Jillian added. "A place that proves strength can emerge from loss."

Aidan nodded, his gaze distant. "And it's a testament to the courage of those who defended it. Even in defeat, they allowed others to survive."

Skaros smiled. "You understand. That's good. But I've saved the most interesting discovery for last. Follow me."

Skaros led them to a hidden passage in the central keep, descending into a network of tunnels beneath the citadel. The air grew cooler as they ventured into the labyrinth, and Aidan's excitement grew. He had missed the thrill of dungeoneering.

The tunnels were a mix of storage areas, living quarters, and ancient catacombs. They passed racks of finely crafted weapons and armour, preserved through the ages. Though mundane in nature, the quality of the craftsmanship was remarkable. Skaros explained that magical wards had protected these subterranean chambers, keeping them intact even as the surface world crumbled.

"The Argar who overran the citadel never dared venture down here," Skaros said. "The wards would have destroyed them. It took our scholars years to decipher the glyphs and safely remove the protections."

In one chamber, Skaros gestured to a massive pillar carved with hieroglyphs. "We call this the Chamber of Treasures. It once held ingots of a red, glass-like substance we now know as Kheferu. This material was crucial in forging weapons against Izen'draazt's forces during the Darkness. Much of the Kheferu, along with gold and platinum, has been returned to our homeland in Kharadia."

Aidan's attention was drawn to the hieroglyphs. "Has this been fully deciphered?" he asked.

"Not entirely," Skaros admitted.

Stepping closer, Aidan began to study the inscriptions. They depicted scenes of snake-like creatures and Adeni worshipping the sun. In other carvings, Adeni were shown trading with Aystar.

Aidan's eyes narrowed as he recognised a name: Hapt-Sept-Amun.

"This name," he said, tracing the glyph with his finger. "It's familiar. He was a king in the Tahnaar Desert, near Kanarzand. These hieroglyphs suggest he was Adeni once, before becoming the undead tyrant we know from history."

Skaros listened intently. "What else do you see?"

"These carvings seem to depict an alliance," Aidan said. "The Adeni, led by Hapt-Sept-Amun, worked alongside the Aystar to combat a common enemy: the snake people, the Zar'tul."

Jillian stepped forward, her eyes scanning the pillar. "This changes how we view history. It wasn't just conflict - there was cooperation."

Aidan nodded. "It shows that even in ancient times, survival depended on unity."

Skaros looked impressed. "This is invaluable," he said. "We've always focused on the Argar as our primary adversaries. But this suggests a broader history, one of alliances and struggles beyond our understanding."

Aidan shared what he knew of Hapt-Sept-Amun from his time in Kanarzand. "The Aystar must have known him before his fall. When I studied the ruins of his city, it was clear he had once been a powerful and respected leader."

The conversation left Skaros deep in thought. "We must investigate further," he said, signalling to his warriors. "Inform the scholars. This is a story that needs to be told."

For the rest of the day, they explored the labyrinth, uncovering more relics and inscriptions. Aidan felt a renewed sense of purpose. The Kale Khestari were beginning to see the value of history beyond the battlefield, and he was proud to be part of that shift. Skaros, too, seemed more open-minded than the other commanders Aidan had encountered, willing to embrace the past as a source of strength rather than merely a reminder of loss.

As they returned to the surface, the desert sun cast long shadows over Kale Khaestas. Aidan looked back at the towering citadel and the labyrinth below, feeling a deep connection to the land and its history. Here, amidst the sands and stone, the past was alive and its lessons would shape the future.

23

An Ominous Feeling

The companions ate well as honoured guests, the warmth of their hosts contrasting sharply with the vast, cold desert that loomed beyond the citadel walls. Rest came easily that night, the fortress's solid stone and the steady hum of patrols offering a sense of safety.

The next morning, a knock sounded at Aidan's door. He opened it to find Jillian, her expression grave, her lavender and gold-flecked eyes shadowed with worry.

"I fear we are not alone," she said, stepping inside. Aidan gestured for her to continue, and she took a deep breath before explaining. "I can sense the presence of the Zealots nearby. They haven't breached the citadel, but they're close. They could assume any form; a person, an animal, even a shadow. Their goal is clear. They want me dead. They want to extinguish my light."

Aidan studied her as she spoke, noting the tension in her voice. Jillian was strong, her resolve forged in the crucible of countless battles, but there was a weariness to her now.

"The Aspiring Dream doesn't tolerate Light speakers. I am hope to my people, and that makes me dangerous to them," she continued. "They will stop at nothing, Aidan. Even now, they're planning the quickest way to kill me and leave no trace."

Aidan frowned, his mind racing. "We can't let them infiltrate the keep. If they do, they could sow deception and chaos among the war band." He tapped a finger against his chin. "Let's tell Ahlissa what you're sensing. Then you and I could take a walk to the temple, just the two of us. It might draw them out."

Jillian raised an eyebrow. "A trap?"

"Not exactly," Aidan said. "More like an invitation. If we're careful, Ahlissa can have her people observe discreetly. If the Zealots show themselves, we deal with them on our terms."

Jillian nodded, her silver hair catching the sunlight streaming through the window. "They might reveal their true forms if they think it'll give them the upper hand. But their target is me. They won't stop unless they think they have a clear shot."

"Good," Aidan said. "Let's get breakfast first. It's going to be a long day."

In the dining hall, Aidan and Jillian enjoyed a meal of fresh fruit and grain bread. Ahlissa joined them, her green eyes sparkling with curiosity.

"What's on today's schedule?" she asked, slicing a piece of citrus fruit. "Anything exciting planned?"

"A possible trap," Aidan replied casually.

Ahlissa paused mid-bite. "Really? Does Skaros know about this?"

"No, and that's intentional," Aidan said. "Jillian senses the Zealots nearby. If we're going to draw them out, we can't risk anyone's identity being compromised. They could mimic any of the Kale Khestari warriors or scholars. We need a small group - just the four of us. That way, if they show themselves, we'll know exactly who we're dealing with."

Ahlissa leaned back in her chair, considering. "Very well. I'll go with you. And I'll bring Cavin Shivohtas. He's my Head of Guard aboard the Zephyr Breeze and one of my most trusted fighters."

Aidan nodded, satisfied. "Then we stick together, no separation. We'll give Skaros a plausible reason for our outing and let the Zealots make their move."

Ahlissa grinned. "I'll handle Skaros. He trusts me implicitly. I'll tell him we're taking a sightseeing trip to the temple. No escorts needed. Give me five minutes."

When she returned, her smile confirmed her success. "Skaros is unconcerned. We're free to go."

By mid-morning, the companions set out, their horses kicking up clouds of sand as they made their way toward the temple. The journey was uneventful at first, the landscape shifting from windswept dunes to jagged outcroppings of sandstone.

Aidan broke the silence. "Jillian, can the Zealots read your mind? Or do they detect you in other ways?"

"It depends on their proficiency," Jillian said, her voice calm. "Some can probe deeper, attempting to plant or extract thoughts. But I've trained extensively. My defences are strong."

"What if you lowered them, just a little?" Aidan suggested. "Let them sense that this is just an innocent outing. It might tempt them to act."

Jillian gave him a sharp look, then nodded. "I can do that."

As the temple came into view, its smooth stone walls rising from the desert like a mirage, Ahlissa leaned forward in her saddle. "It's smaller than I expected," she said.

"It's more in line with Hapt-Sept-Amun's culture," Aidan noted. "Perhaps a place of alliance between his people and the Aystar settlers."

"Fascinating," Ahlissa murmured.

The avenue leading to the temple was flanked by statues of sphinxes, their enigmatic faces weathered by centuries of sandstorms. At the end of the avenue stood a large entrance, framed by statues, their features unmistakably Adeni and Aystaran.

Inside, the air was cool and faintly sweet, carrying the scent of ancient stone and something indefinable yet soothing. The group moved through side chambers and narrow halls, eventually arriving in the main worship chamber.

The chamber was dominated by a central altar, behind which a carved sunburst seemed to radiate light, though no torches burned. Statues of significant Aystaran deities and three Adeni figures - Set, Apep, and Sobek - stood vigil around the space. Hieroglyphs adorned every surface, their meaning waiting to be unravelled.

"This place is remarkable," Aidan said, his voice tinged with awe. "A true testament to the alliance between two ancient peoples."

Jillian nodded, tracing her fingers over the carvings. "There's no hint of their common enemy here, though. No snakes, no Zar'tul. Strange, isn't it?"

"Perhaps the alliance was forged in hope, not fear," Ahlissa suggested.

Cavin, the guard, chuckled. "I hate snakes. Let's hope they stay out of this fight."

For hours, Aidan studied the inscriptions, piecing together fragments of a long-lost history. The temple seemed to hum with latent energy, and the companions noticed small cuts and bruises healing rapidly.

"Do you sense the Zealots?" Aidan asked Jillian as she meditated near the altar.

Her eyes snapped open, silver light flickering within. "They're close. Very close."

A sudden gust of wind sent sand swirling through the entranceway, and the sound of howling grew louder. Ahlissa stood, her hand on her blade. "That storm wasn't there before."

"It's not their doing," Jillian said, her voice steady. "But they're using it. Stay close, and don't lose sight of each other. They're inside now."

Aidan retrieved an enchanted lantern from his pack and activated it, its light revealing hidden auras. As the four companions moved toward an antechamber, leading to a courtyard, shadows began to lengthen unnaturally, and the air grew heavy with tension.

"Stay sharp," Aidan warned. "This is where they'll strike."

24

The Sand Storm

The sandstorm arrived with a ferocity that reduced the horizon to a swirling, beige oblivion. The wind roared through the citadel's battlements, and the sand clawed at any exposed surface. Inside the ruined Sun Tower complex, the Kale Khestari had sealed the fortress, heavy stone doors grinding shut against the onslaught. Despite the protection, the storm's howl permeated the air, setting nerves on edge.

Aidan stood with Jillian and Ahlissa in the main courtyard, their eyes fixed on the whirling chaos outside the arrow slits. The storm was ominous, but it wasn't just the weather that had the group tense.

"This could be the opportunity the Zealots are waiting for," Jillian said, her voice low and steady despite the gale outside. "The storm masks their movements. The Zealots - possessed by the Sah'ren - are immune to such inconveniences; they're guided by their parasitic masters and their will. We must be ready."

Aidan's hand hovered near the hilt of his sword, and Ahlissa nodded grimly. They had prepared for this moment, but anticipation coiled in their chests like a living thing. The Zealots- fanatical agents of The Aspiring Dream - were relentless in their pursuit of Jillian. They would not stop until she was either captured or dead.

The first sign of their arrival was subtle, almost imperceptible. A faint shimmer in the air, like the distorted image of a mirage, formed near the edge of the courtyard. Then, stepping through the haze, came a figure of undeniable beauty and menace.

The woman was tall and slender, her violet eyes shimmering with an eerie, otherworldly light. Her flowing black hair, held back by an intricate headpiece, cascaded down her back like a waterfall of night. Loose robes of deep blue and purple twisted with living patterns, as though the fabric itself pulsed with hidden power. In one hand, she held a crystalline crossbow aimed directly at Jillian.

"Surrender, Khystar," the woman commanded, her voice silken and unyielding. "Do not be afraid. The folly of your ancestors is not your fault, but you must return to us. Accept your fate and embrace the Dark. The Aspiring Dream is restless. Your spirit is fractured; we can restore it."

Jillian's lips tightened into a thin line. Her body was still, but her eyes burned with defiance. "Never. I follow the Path of the Light. You will not take that from me."

In an instant, Jillian transformed. Her figure shifted to one of radiant beauty, rivalling the Zealot's grace but imbued with a celestial glow. Loose trousers and a halter top shimmered on her frame, her bracers pulsing with faint light. Her flowing hair turned into a cascade of red, gold, and silver, wild and untamed. Silver light radiated from her brilliant eyes, and in her upturned palms, two slender blades of glowing silver materialized. She shifted into a defensive stance, her entire being a beacon of defiance.

The Zealot's smile was cold. "The Light speakers were weak. We crushed them when we invaded your sanctuary in Aldrosia. Give up now, and your passing will be painless. Resistance is futile."

"Never," Jillian spat. Her voice rose with conviction. "You can never extinguish the flames of vengeance that burn within the Khystar!"

The Zealot chuckled, a chilling sound that sent a shiver down Aidan's spine. "You have much to learn, renegade," she said. "The Circle of Dark has willed this moment, and we are not so easily defeated."

As if on cue, soft footfalls echoed through the swirling storm outside. Shadows coalesced, and four more figures emerged, each as imposing and sinister as the first. They stepped with unnerving precision, surrounding Aidan, Jillian, and Ahlissa.

The air grew heavy with an oppressive aura, thick with malice and dark intent. Aidan felt his breath hitch, and an involuntary wave of fear coursed through him. The Zealots' presence was unnatural, a distortion of the world that gnawed at his resolve.

Ahlissa stepped closer to him, her voice steady but low. "Hold your ground. They want us to break first."

The Zealots moved as one, forming a tightening circle around their quarry. Each bore crystalline weapons, their forms unnaturally poised, like predators toying with their prey. The leader kept her crossbow trained on Jillian, but her violet eyes flicked briefly to Aidan and Ahlissa.

"This need not concern you," she said, her voice smooth as silk. "We seek only the renegade. Leave her to us, and you will be unharmed."

Aidan's grip tightened on his sword. "You're mistaken if you think we'll hand her over."

The leader's eyes narrowed. "Foolish. You court your own destruction."

The stand-off was broken in a flash of silver and violet. Jillian moved first, her radiant blades a blur as she closed the distance to the lead Zealot. Her strike was swift and precise, aimed at disarming her opponent.

The Zealot responded with equal speed, her crystalline crossbow snapping up to fire a bolt of searing purple energy. Jillian deflected the projectile with a spinning slash, the impact sparking brightly in the dim light of the sandstorm.

Aidan leapt into action, his sword drawn and ready. He lunged at one of the other Zealots, forcing the enemy back with a flurry of calculated strikes. The Zealot moved unnaturally, dodging with inhuman speed and countering with a whip-like weapon that glowed faintly with dark energy. Aidan parried, feeling the force of the attack vibrate through his arms.

Ahlissa joined the fray, her hands weaving intricate patterns in the air as she cast a shimmering protective barrier around herself and her allies. The barrier flared brightly as it deflected an incoming bolt of energy, dissipating the attack harmlessly into the air.

The courtyard erupted into chaos, the storm outside providing an eerie backdrop to the battle.

As Aidan fought, he couldn't shake the oppressive aura emanating from the Zealots. Each movement felt heavier, each breath a struggle against the intense darkness that clung to the air. But he pushed forward, his strikes growing more forceful with each clash.

The Zealot before him faltered momentarily, and Aidan seized the opportunity. He feinted left before driving his sword upward in a powerful arc, slicing through the crystalline whip. The weapon shattered with a sharp crack, and the Zealot hissed in frustration, retreating a step.

Jillian's battle was far more dazzling. Her glowing blades danced like streaks of silver lightning, her every motion fluid and purposeful. She clashed with the leader, the two locked in a deadly duel that sent flashes of light and energy cascading across the courtyard.

The Zealot leader's composure wavered, her graceful strikes growing desperate. "You cannot win, Khystar," she snarled. "You fight against the will of the Dream itself!"

Jillian's reply was a fierce cry of defiance as her blades crashed against the Zealot's weapon, sending shards of crystalline energy scattering.

With a sharp command from their leader, the remaining Zealots regrouped, their movements unnervingly coordinated. They formed a defensive formation, their weapons glowing ominously as they prepared a combined attack.

"They're preparing something big!" Ahlissa warned, her voice cutting through the storm's howl. She raised her hands, channelling energy into a shimmering dome of light that enveloped her companions.

Aidan braced himself, his eyes darting between the Zealots as the oppressive energy in the air intensified. "Jillian, now's the time to end this!" he shouted.

Jillian surged forward, her radiant form blazing as she unleashed a flurry of devastating strikes. Her blades carved through the Zealots' defences, their coordinated attack faltering under her relentless assault. One by one, the Zealots fell, their forms dissolving into shimmering motes of dark energy that were carried away by the storm.

The leader was the last to fall, her defiance turning to desperation as Jillian's blades struck true. With a final cry, the Zealot disintegrated, leaving only silence in her wake.

As the storm began to subside, the courtyard was left eerily quiet. Jillian stood at the centre, her glowing blades fading as she exhaled heavily. Aidan and Ahlissa approached her, their expressions a mixture of relief and admiration.

"You did it," Aidan said, clapping a hand on her shoulder.

Jillian nodded, her silver eyes still glinting faintly. "The Dream sent their hunters, but they will find no peace here. Not while the Light endures."

Ahlissa surveyed the scene, her gaze sharp. "This was a victory, but it won't be the last time they come for you. We need to remain vigilant."

Aidan sheathed his sword, his resolve firm. "Let them come. We'll be ready."

25

The Aspiring Dream

Jillian collapsed to her knees, the aftermath of the battle taking its toll. Tears streamed freely down her cheeks as she clasped her hands in a gesture of prayer, her voice trembling as she whispered words of gratitude and hope. Her sobs quieted, and she looked up at Aidan and Ahlissa with a fragile smile.

"For now, I am safe," she said softly, her voice carrying a bittersweet note. "But I know more will come. They'll never stop. When these five fail to report back, The Aspiring Dream will send others."

Aidan stepped closer and placed a reassuring hand on her shoulder. "Let them come. We'll face them together."

The fallen Zealots lay scattered around the temple's desecrated worship chamber. One by one, their bodies began to change. From the eyes, ears, nose, and mouth of each corpse, a glowing mist escaped, twisting into the air like tendrils of spectral smoke. A strange, mournful wail accompanied the departure of the Sah'ren spirits, their otherworldly presence lingering for just a moment before dissipating into nothingness.

The lifeless vessels remained in place for a single eerie moment. They were tall, elegant, and hauntingly beautiful, but the perfection was short-lived. Within seconds, their forms began to decay at an unnatural rate. Skin shrivelled and cracked, bones turned to dust, and clothing and equipment disintegrated as though consumed by invisible flames. By the end of a single minute, nothing remained but empty patches of ground.

Jillian shuddered at the sight, unable to look away. "They're nothing without their masters. Just tools, discarded when they fail."

Ahlissa nodded grimly. "Tools or not, they were dangerous. This proves they weren't acting alone."

The temple returned to its unsettling quiet. The howling sandstorm outside was the only sound that broke the oppressive stillness. Aidan surveyed the room, his hand still gripping his sword as he waited for any signs of lingering danger. When none came, he exhaled and lowered his weapon.

"We should regroup," he said, nodding toward the main worship chamber.

They made their way back, their footsteps echoing in the hollow corridors of the temple. As they entered the chamber, a sense of calm washed over them. The room seemed to radiate a subtle energy, soothing their wounds and restoring their strength.

Aidan flexed his fingers, surprised to feel the aches and pains of the battle melting away. Jillian looked similarly rejuvenated, the exhaustion in her eyes replaced by her solid determination.

"Thank you," Jillian said, her voice steady but filled with emotion. "Thank you for believing in my cause and standing by me."

"It was our pleasure," Ahlissa replied warmly. "The Aystaran people have always stood against those who seek to corrupt and dominate. Groups like The Aspiring Dream have no place in Scylla."

Aidan nodded in agreement. "Your fight is our fight. The Zealots will find no victory here."

When they finally stepped outside, the sandstorm had begun to wane, though its aftermath was evident. The desert around the temple was scoured clean, the swirling winds having erased all traces of footprints or travel. The air was heavy with the lingering scent of sand and ozone, and the heat shimmered in waves across the endless dunes.

Ahlissa scanned the landscape, her sharp eyes assessing the terrain. "They must have arrived on a ship," she mused. "The storm has wiped out any signs of how they got here, but there's only one logical place to start."

She gestured toward a narrow, twisting path that led up the sandstone cliffs flanking the temple. The path was carved into the cliffside, a precarious route that wound through jagged outcrops and loose gravel.

"We'll take the high ground and see what's out there," Ahlissa decided. She led the way, her confident strides showing no hesitation. Aidan followed close behind, with Jillian bringing up the rear.

The climb was not long, but the shifting sands and the uneven footing made it treacherous. As they ascended, the wind tugged at their clothes, and the sun beat down mercilessly. Finally, they reached the top, where the desert stretched out before them in an unbroken expanse of golden dunes and rocky outcroppings.

The view from the cliffs was both beautiful and desolate. The desert seemed endless, its vastness broken only by the faint shimmer of heat mirages that danced on the horizon. Aidan shielded his eyes and scanned the landscape, searching for anything unusual.

"There," Ahlissa said, pulling an eyeglass from her belt. She raised it to her eye and focused on a faint glint of light far in the distance.

"What do you see?" Jillian asked, stepping closer.

Ahlissa adjusted the eyeglass, her expression growing serious. "There's an airship out there," she confirmed. "Small, likely the transport for the Aldrosian agents."

"How far out?" Aidan asked.

"About two hours on horseback," Ahlissa replied, lowering the eyeglass. "But if I were its captain, I wouldn't stick around for that long."

"Can you tell who it belongs to?" Jillian asked.

Ahlissa frowned. "Its design is familiar. It could be Sindarri. If that's the case, Mhorvaeus might be involved. Or it could be a mission sponsored by the Sceptre Guilds."

Aidan clenched his fists. "Either way, we need to investigate. If that ship's still there, it might have answers - or more enemies."

26

Determination

Ahlissa considered the options, her mind working quickly. "We can't afford to spend the time on horseback, and the storm's left the terrain unstable. But we could use the Zephyr Breeze to close the distance. It's faster and gives us the element of surprise."

Jillian nodded. "And if they're still there, we can ensure they don't report back to Aldrosia."

Aidan agreed. "Let's move quickly. The longer we wait, the greater the chance they escape."

The group descended the cliffs with haste, the urgency of their mission driving them forward. By the time they reached the temple's entrance, the Kale Khestari warriors were already preparing the Zephyr Breeze for departure, heeding Ahlissa's earlier orders.

Ahlissa took command, issuing instructions with precision. "Ready the ship for immediate launch. We're heading for the coordinates I provide. Be prepared for combat; it's likely we'll encounter resistance."

The crew sprang into action, their movements efficient and disciplined. Aidan and Jillian joined the preparations, checking their weapons and ensuring they were ready for whatever awaited them.

As the Zephyr Breeze lifted into the air, the vast desert unfolded below them. The storm had cleared entirely, leaving the sands smooth and shimmering under the midday sun. Ahlissa stood at the helm, her eyes fixed on the horizon as she directed the ship toward the distant glint of light.

Aidan stood beside her, scanning the landscape with his own keen eyes. "If it's Sindarri, they'll have protocols for retreat," he said. "We'll need to strike fast before they can signal for reinforcements."

Jillian joined them, her expression resolute. "They'll know we're coming. The Zealots always do. But this time, we're ready."

The Zephyr Breeze surged forward, cutting through the air with precision.

The Zephyr Breeze soared over the dunes, its sails catching the steady desert winds. Below, the sun blazed mercilessly, turning the sands into an undulating ocean of heat and light. Ahlissa stood at the helm, her posture rigid with determination as she steered toward the distant speck of the airship.

"It's stationary," she noted. "They're either waiting for something or hiding."

Aidan leaned on the railing, his sharp eyes fixed on the target. "If it's stationary, we have the upper hand. We strike before they can react."

Jillian joined them, her face set with grim resolve. "This could be a trap. The Sah'ren are masters of deceit."

Ahlissa nodded. "A valid concern, but we've come too far to turn back. Ready the crew. I want everyone at their stations."

The Zephyr Breeze crested another dune, and the distant airship came into clearer view. It was small, sleek, and unmistakably of Sindarri design. The hull glimmered faintly in the sunlight, its polished surface betraying a level of sophistication that hinted at its origins.

As the Zephyr Breeze closed the distance, the Sindarri vessel showed no signs of movement. It remained anchored in a shallow valley between dunes, almost blending with the terrain. Ahlissa slowed their approach, signalling the crew to ready the weapons.

"Something's not right," Aidan murmured, his hand instinctively moving to the hilt of his sword. "Why aren't they reacting?"

Jillian narrowed her eyes. "They know we're coming. They want us to think we have the advantage."

Suddenly, a flash of movement caught Aidan's attention. "There! Along the dunes!"

A dozen figures emerged from the sands, their forms obscured by flowing desert robes. They moved with unnatural speed, their robes billowing around them like shadows given life.

"Aldrosian agents," Jillian hissed.

Ahlissa barked orders. "Crew to arms! Prepare for ground assault!"

The Zealots charged, their weapons glinting as they closed the distance with inhuman speed. Aidan, Jillian, and Ahlissa leaped to the sand below, weapons drawn as they braced for the attack.

The first wave of Zealot agents struck with ferocity. Aidan met their charge head-on, his sword clashing against a pair of jagged black daggers wielded by one of the Sah'ren vessels. The agent's movements were fast, almost erratic, but Aidan's training and reflexes allowed him to keep pace.

Jillian danced through the fray, her glowing silver blades weaving a deadly pattern of light. She parried a strike aimed at her heart and countered with a precise slash that sent her opponent sprawling.

Ahlissa stood her ground, her long spear flashing as she drove back two attackers at once. Her movements were deliberate, each thrust and sweep of her weapon perfectly calculated.

Despite their skill, the Sah'ren pressed hard, their supernatural strength and agility pushing the companions to their limits. For every agent that fell, another seemed to emerge from the shifting sands.

"They're trying to wear us down!" Jillian shouted, her voice strained as she deflected another attack.

"We won't let them!" Aidan growled, driving his sword through the chest of an advancing agent.

Ahlissa shouted an order to the crew aboard the Zephyr Breeze. "Now! Fire at will!"

The ship's mounted ballistae loosed a barrage of explosive bolts, striking the sand around the Zealots and scattering their formation. The blasts sent shock waves through the battlefield, giving the companions a momentary reprieve.

Aidan used the chaos to his advantage, pressing the attack against the nearest agent. With a powerful swing, he disarmed his opponent and followed with a decisive strike that ended the fight.

Jillian, her movements fuelled by a mix of fury and determination, unleashed a series of strikes that left her final opponent staggered and defeated.

The Sah'ren began to falter, their numbers dwindling rapidly under the combined assault of the companions and the Zephyr Breeze's crew.

As the battle subsided, the Sindarri airship finally roared to life, its engines humming with power. The sleek vessel began to lift off, its captain attempting to escape the carnage.

"Not so fast," Ahlissa muttered. She fuelled to the Zephyr Breeze, which fired a grappling hook that latched onto the Sindarri ship's hull.

The companions boarded the Sindarri vessel, climbing aboard with practiced ease. Inside, the ship's captain, a wiry man with sharp features and cold eyes, stood at the helm.

"You've made a mistake coming here," he snarled, drawing a slim, wickedly curved blade.

"No," Aidan replied, his voice low and steady. "You did when you thought you could threaten us."

The captain lunged, his movements swift and deadly, but Aidan was ready. Their blades clashed, the sound ringing through the narrow cabin. Jillian and Ahlissa flanked the captain, cutting off his escape routes.

With a final, well-placed strike, Aidan disarmed the captain and knocked him to the ground.

The companions secured the Sindarri ship and began searching for clues. In the captain's quarters, they found detailed maps of the desert, marked with routes and notes that suggested the Aldrosian agents' movements had been carefully planned.

"This was no random mission," Ahlissa said, scanning the documents. "They've been tracking Jillian for weeks."

Jillian frowned. "They won't stop until I'm dead or captured."

"They won't get the chance," Aidan said firmly.

Among the maps, Aidan found a cryptic note written in elegant script. The message mentioned a meeting with Mhorvaeus and hinted at a deeper conspiracy involving The Sceptre Guilds and the Council of Thirteen in Gideon City.

"This isn't over," Aidan said, tucking the note into his pouch. "I fear a wider war is planned."

27

The Blooded

Aidan prompted Ahlissa with urgency, "Do you remember the conversation I told you about in Cordovar with Matax?"

"Yes," Ahlissa nodded, her sharp gaze narrowing.

"We have an opportunity now to strike Mhorvaeus' followers with an element of surprise," Aidan continued. "Matax was certain that a gathering was going to take place; a group known as The Blooded."

Jillian, her resolve unshaken, spoke firmly. "I'm in. Aidan is right. We should take this fight to them now and end it. I don't want to keep running."

"Can you recall where to find it?" Ahlissa asked.

"Yes," Aidan replied, his tone edged with determination. "We need to follow an old trade route north from Cordovar, past a place named the City of Ash. If we look for a monolith shaped like a crescent; it marks the entrance to a hidden path."

Ahlissa nodded decisively. "Then let's prepare the Zephyr Breeze. We'll get there as fast as we can. But we'll need more than brute force - we'll need strategy. If Mhorvaeus is there, he won't be alone, and The Blooded will be expecting resistance."

The Zephyr Breeze soared over the wasteland, its shadow trailing across dunes and ash-laden plains. The once-thriving City of Ash was now little more than ruins, a stark reminder of Scylla's tumultuous history. The airship's sleek frame cut through the dusty winds as Ahlissa barked orders to her crew, ensuring the vessel remained on high alert.

Aidan stood at the bow, studying a crumbling map Matax had given him. The crescent monolith loomed in his thoughts. According to Matax, it was both a marker and a warning - a place few dared to approach.

The Zephyr Breeze hovered over the barren wasteland as twilight fell, casting long shadows across the sands. The crescent-shaped monolith loomed against the horizon like a jagged relic of another age, its dark stone gleaming faintly in the dying light. The air was thick with anticipation as the ship touched down a safe distance away.

"This is it," Aidan said, gripping the hilt of his sword as they disembarked. "The path Matax mentioned should be just beyond the monolith." Aidan's lantern, enchanted to reveal hidden paths, illuminated faint glyphs carved into the stone.

Jillian's gaze darted toward the looming structure, her expression a mix of awe and apprehension. "I can feel the tension in the air. It's like this place is holding its breath."

Elira Veylin, the New Kanarzand Bureau of Forbidden Archaeology's expert on magical inscriptions, approached the monolith, her fingers tracing the ancient glyphs etched into its surface. "These runes are fascinating," she murmured. "They speak of gateways and thresholds. Sacrifice and rebirth. It's more than a marker - it's a key."

Malrik Fenhal, the New Kanarzand Bureau of Forbidden Archaeology's planar specialist, stood still and watched cautiously. "I can feel a powerful presence here," he warned them. "We have experienced this before. Izen'draazt. The damn fools are trying to summon him!"

Renlor Drax, the New Kanarzand Bureau of Forbidden Archaeology's tactician and tracker, knelt beside the base of the monolith, studying the ground intently. "There's been a lot of movement here recently. Footsteps, carts, and some heavy dragging. They've been bringing something big through here."

Ahlissa motioned for the group to gather. "We move carefully from here. The Blooded will have defences in place. Renlor, you take point. Elira, watch for magical traps. Everyone else, stay alert."

The path behind the monolith descended into a narrow canyon, its walls etched with weathered carvings of long-forgotten figures. The deeper they ventured, the more oppressive the atmosphere became. The air grew colder, carrying faint whispers that seemed to emanate from the stone itself.

"They've tampered with something ancient here," Elira said, her voice low as she examined a glowing glyph along the wall. "These wards were meant to keep something in - or keep something out."

"They're using it for their ritual," Aidan guessed. "Mhorvaeus doesn't care about the consequences as long as he gets what he wants."

The group emerged into a wide cavern, its floor littered with the remnants of old trade routes: broken wheels, rusted chains, and fragments of shattered crates. At the far end, a massive stone door stood ajar, revealing a faint, pulsating red light beyond.

"That's not ominous at all," Renlor muttered.

Aidan motioned for the group to halt. "This is it. Beyond that door is the temple. Be ready for anything."

The air inside the temple was stifling, thick with the scent of burning incense and something metallic. Flickering torches lined the walls, casting eerie shadows that danced like restless spirits. The central chamber was vast, dominated by a massive device of alien design. It was a construct of interlocking black metal and glowing red veins, pulsating like a living heart.

At the base of the device stood Mhorvaeus, his purple robes billowing as he addressed a gathering of crimson robed figures. His voice echoed through the chamber, rich with fervour. "The time has come! The shard's power will tear the veil, and we shall ascend as rulers of this new world!"

Aidan's stomach tightened as he spotted another amber coloured Aethyr shard, its dark energy radiating from the heart of the device. It pulsed in time with the machine, each thrum sending waves of energy through the room.

Malrik leaned closer to Ahlissa, whispering urgently. "That device is a planar rift generator. If he activates it fully, it will open a portal to the Void. The Blooded want to merge this realm with the Void's chaos."

"Not on my watch," Ahlissa hissed, her pistols already drawn.

Aidan stepped forward, his voice cutting through the ritual's din. "Mhorvaeus! It ends here!"

The cult leader turned, his glowing eyes narrowing in recognition. "Ah, Aidan. Always meddling where you don't belong. You and your rabble are too late. The shard has already begun its work."

Jillian moved beside Aidan, her energy blades forming with a metallic hum. "You've preyed on my people long enough, Mhorvaeus. This ends now."

Mhorvaeus sneered. "You cannot comprehend the power we are unleashing. The Twelve understood the necessity of control, but they lacked the vision. I will succeed where they failed."

Ahlissa raised her pistols. "Then let's see how your vision holds up against reality."

With a sharp gesture, Mhorvaeus unleashed a wave of dark energy. The group scattered as the ground beneath them cracked and erupted with shadowy tendrils. The cultists surged forward, weapons drawn, chanting as they attacked.

Aidan met the first cultist head-on, his blade cutting through the air in a flash of steel. The robed figure fell, but another took their place, swinging a jagged blade crackling with dark magic. Jillian moved like a dancer, her glowing blades carving through enemies with precise, fluid motions.

Renlor and Cavin took up defensive positions, firing arrows and crossbow bolts at the advancing cultists. Elira worked furiously at the edge of the chamber, her hands tracing intricate patterns as she attempted to disrupt the rift generator's enchantments.

"Mhorvaeus!" Ahlissa shouted, firing shot after shot at the cult leader. He deflected the bullets with a shield of crackling energy, his laughter echoing through the chamber.

"You are but insects before the storm!" Mhorvaeus bellowed, raising his hands to the shard. The device flared, the rift above it expanding into a swirling vortex of red and black.

"Aidan!" Malrik shouted over the chaos. "We can't destroy the generator outright - it'll collapse the rift and take us with it! We need to sever its connection to the shard first!"

Aidan nodded, his mind racing. "Jillian! Can you use your light to disrupt the shard?"

"I'll try!" she replied, darting toward the dais. Her blades vanished as she raised her hands, channelling radiant energy toward the shard. The dark crystal resisted, flaring brighter as it clashed with her power.

Aidan stood at the edge of the expanding rift, his heart pounding as he stared into its swirling depths. Tendrils of dark energy reached out, trying to ensnare him in their grasp. He could feel Izen'draazt's presence growing stronger, whispering promises of unimaginable power and secrets long buried. The demon's voice was seductive, filling Aidan's mind with visions of himself as a ruler, commanding legions and reshaping Scylla to his will.

"*Aidan,*" the demon's voice echoed, "*with your Aethyr Mark, you can stabilize the rift. Imagine the power you will wield, the knowledge you will uncover. You could control the very fate of Scylla. Allow me to show you the truth about your lineage, the final fate of the Kale Ashtari.*"

Aidan's hand hovered over the glowing mark on his forearm, torn between the temptation of Izen'draazt's offer and the warnings of his companions. His thoughts were interrupted by Jillian's urgent voice.

"Don't listen to him, Aidan!" she called out, her voice cutting through the dark whispers. She stepped forward, placing a reassuring hand on his shoulder. "I've faced the darkness of Aldrosia before. It's alluring, but it's a trap. You have the power to choose your own path, to forge your own destiny."

Aidan hesitated, glancing back at Jillian. Her eyes were filled with determination and a hint of fear for him. He knew she spoke from experience, having battled her own demons and emerged stronger for it. Her words resonated with him, giving him the strength to resist the pull of Izen'draazt's influence.

Ahlissa joined them, her gaze calm and steady. "Understanding your history is important, Aidan, but it doesn't have to define your future. You are more than your lineage. You have the potential to create a new legacy, one that is shaped by your choices, not by the shadows of the past."

The ground beneath them trembled as the rift continued to widen. Dark tendrils lashed out, striking at Aidan and his companions. Aidan raised his sword, channelling his energy to create a protective barrier. The tendrils recoiled, hissing in frustration.

"I won't be your pawn, Izen'draazt!" Aidan shouted, his voice resolute. "I will find my own way, without your twisted guidance."

The demon's laughter echoed through the air, mockingly. *"You think you can resist me, boy? The rift is already consuming you. Your precious Scylla will fall, and there is nothing you can do to stop it."*

Aidan's grip tightened on his sword. He glanced at Jillian and Ahlissa, drawing strength from their unwavering support. With a determined cry, he charged forward, plunging his sword into the heart of the rift. The blade glowed with a brilliant light, pushing back the darkness.

The rift shuddered, its edges beginning to close. Izen'draazt's enraged roar filled the air, but Aidan did not falter. He focused all his energy on sealing the rift, refusing to let the demon's influence take hold.

Beside him, Jillian unleashed her magic, creating barriers to protect them from the rift's violent convulsions. Ahlissa channelled her own power, reinforcing Aidan's efforts. Together, they fought against the encroaching darkness, their combined strength proving greater than the sum of their individual abilities.

Slowly but surely, the rift began to shrink, its power waning. Izen'draazt's presence grew weaker, his influence fading. Aidan felt a surge of hope and determination. He would not be controlled by the demon.

Mhorvaeus snarled, turning his focus to Jillian. "You will not interfere!"

He thrust his hand forward, sending a bolt of shadow hurtling toward her. Aidan intercepted it, his blade glowing with light as he deflected the attack. "You'll have to go through me first."

Aidan and Mhorvaeus clashed in the centre of the chamber, their powers colliding in bursts of light and shadow. The cult leader fought with a ferocity born of desperation, but Aidan's resolve burned brighter. Each strike of his blade chipped away at Mhorvaeus' defences, his shield faltering under the relentless assault.

Behind them, Jillian's light finally pierced the shard's defences. With a brilliant flash, the shard's connection to the generator shattered. The rift above it wavered, its swirling chaos beginning to collapse.

"No!" Mhorvaeus roared, his eyes wide with fury. "You cannot undo what has been set in motion!"

Ahlissa fired a final shot, the bullet striking true. Mhorvaeus staggered, his shield failing entirely. Aidan seized the moment, driving his blade through the cult leader's chest. Mhorvaeus' scream echoed through the chamber as his body disintegrated into ash, his essence consumed by the collapsing rift.

The chamber fell silent as the rift sealed completely, leaving only the lifeless shard and the smouldering remains of the generator. The surviving cultists fled into the shadows, their will broken with Mhorvaeus' death.

Elira approached the shard cautiously, her hands glowing with containment magic. "It's inert now, but still dangerous. We need to secure it."

"Izen'draazt is defeated," Malrik informed everyone. "I cannot sense him any longer. We have succeeded in thwarting Mhorvaeus's sinister plans."

Ahlissa holstered her pistols, her expression weary but victorious. "Let's get it to the New Kanarzand Bureau of Forbidden Archaeology."

* * *

As the companions returned to the Zephyr Breeze, the desert winds began to die down, leaving the sands eerily still. The sun dipped low on the horizon, casting long shadows across the dunes.

Jillian stood at the ship's railing, gazing out at the vast expanse of desert. "I'll never stop fighting," she said softly. "As long as I breathe, I'll stand against the darkness."

Aidan joined her, his expression resolute. "You're not alone. We'll face whatever comes together."

Ahlissa approached, her voice filled with determination. "We have allies, resources, and the will to resist. Whatever schemes The Aspiring Dream, or The Sceptre Guilds have planned, we'll be ready. For now, we have weakened them."

"And what of Izen'draazt?"

"I doubt we've heard the last from him," Aidan replied. "But for the time being, I feel a calm that hasn't been with me for a long time. His influence over me has gone. This confrontation has rendered my Aethyr Mark inert."

"Until something else triggers it," Ahlissa warned.

"Possibly," Aidan said thoughtfully. "But this time it feels different."

"What are your plans?" Jillian asked him.

"Well, if it's OK with everyone, I'd like to spend some time with the New Kanarzand Bureau of Forbidden Archaeology. Somebody needs to catalogue the remaining Khestar platforms and ensure their power cannot be exploited."

"Can I join you?" Jillian asked. "I know The Aspiring Dream remains in the shadows, hunting for me, but we work well together as a team. You could be my protector."

"I'd like that," Aidan reassured her.

"I want to preserve my people's teachings about the Path of Light."

Aidan smiled, knowing in his heart that they belonged with each other and his expression was one of clarity and purpose. "We'll do that together," he told her.

He clutched an ancient artefact recovered from the monolith, a reminder of both his lineage and his choices. The artefact was small, fitting comfortably in the palm of his hand, yet it exuded an aura of profound significance. It was crafted from a rare, iridescent stone that seemed to shift colours with the light, ranging from deep blues to shimmering golds. Intricate carvings adorned its surface, depicting scenes of celestial beings and long-lost civilisations, their stories etched in delicate lines that told of ancient wisdom and forgotten power.

At its centre, a small, glowing crystal pulsed with a gentle light, resonating with Aidan's own Aethyr Mark. This crystal, believed to be a fragment of a star, was said to hold the memories of the ancestors, a conduit to the past. Holding it, Aidan felt a connection to those who had come before him, their hopes, their battles, their dreams.

The artefact's weight was a comfort, grounding him in the present while linking him to a lineage of guardians and scholars. It was a symbol of his journey and a beacon for his future. For the first time, Aidan felt truly free - not bound by his ancestry but empowered by his understanding of it. The past had given him strength, and the future remained his to forge.

The wind carried Jillian's laughter as Ahlissa steered the ship toward new skies.

Glossary

Aden

One of the major nations in the world of Scylla, formed as a grouping of larger regions that are populated predominantly by the Adeni people.

Adeni

Equivalent to Adeni in common fantasy settings; mostly civilised and users of magic and technology. Some nomadic tribal groups do exist. The Adeni do accept the Argar as workers in cities and towns and engage with the Aystar for politics, trade and academic research.

Aethyr Reaches

A wild, isolated wilderness area that is known for its dense forests, magical creatures, and ancient druidic traditions. Spirit creatures are rumoured to dwell deep in the forests. An ancient and dangerous cult exists here.

Agaria

This is the collective name given to the Agar-controlled territories.

Age of Calamity

This was the Fourth Age. It was a period of time in which all the nations waged bitter warfare against each other. It is also the time when vast natural disasters occurred, including the devastation wrought by a great celestial body from the Eternal Void that led to the fall of the Aystar Kingdom, the destruction of the Argar Empire, the demise of Hapt-Sept Amun's city, and the formation of the Tahnaar Desert and its wider region on the continent of Syrnadar.

Age of Creation

This was the Third Age when the Khestar transitioned to become the Aystar factions of the Kale Khestari and Kale Ashtari. This is also the time when the Aethyric realm of Aldrosia remained to conceal the continued existence of the Khystar in a separate state of reality.

Age of Darkness

This was the First Age when the world of Scylla formed but was dominated and consumed by dark shadowy entities and evil creatures. Aroth, the First Vampire, rose to prominence at this time.

Age of Dreams

This was the Second Age, and it is the period of time when the Khestar and Khystar people arrived from the Eternal Void in their ethereal form and settled in the continent of Kharadia, ultimately harnessing the light strands of Aethyr to manifest and build the physical world.

Age of Rediscovery

This is the Fifth Age. It is the current period of time in which the Adeni,

Aystar and Argar people are tolerant yet mistrustful of one another. The world of Scylla is dominated by many factions and power groups as a result and espionage is commonplace.

Aethyr

This is the primordial, mystical force or energy that provides magic to the world. It exists in positive or negative influence, commonly referenced as light or dark, and manifests in sentient beings as good or evil. The essence of Aethyr can be condensed and stored in crystals and stones, which are used to augment magical spells, imbue special powers into items or activate arcane energy devices.

Ahlissa

The independent captain and resourceful owner of the airship The Zephyr Breeze. A smuggler and opportunist with connections to the Argar, she is poised to become an important player, possibly aiding Aidan in his quest with access to rare resources and information.

Aidan

The main protagonist of the story; a half-Aystar scholar and student of magic. In Kharadia, he gains knowledge from the Keepers of the Past and is trained as an Adept in the Temple of the Ages. In order to prove himself an equal, and to be accepted rather than shunned as an outsider, he also trains in the ways of the Kale Khestari as a warrior.

Airships

There are four significant airships operated by the Aystar across the continents of Kharadia and Syrnadar; the Zephyr Breeze, the Zephyr Cloud, the Zephyr Spirit and the Zephyr Storm. Each is powered by a combination of Aethyr and ancient Khestar technology making them very advanced. Other smaller airships and flying vessels exist, operated by the various organisations, political factions and trade guilds of Scylla.

Aldrosia

A mountain sanctuary for the Khystar people seeking to escape the influence of the Zealots of the Dreamlands.

Alira

Captain of the Zephyr Spirit; a skilled tactician, calm and calculating in times of tension.

Alqabda

An aggressive and powerful faction of Argar Raiders in the Forbidden Waste. Known as "The Fist".

Althas

Captain of the Guard for Lord Mhorvaeus.

Aren Shivaleth

The Ambassador for the Aystaran people, and liaison for their various factions, usually resident at the Aystaran Embassy in Gideon City.

Argar

Equivalent to orcs in common fantasy settings; mostly subservient to Adeni in civilised areas but proud, self-determining and indignant towards all races in their traditional wilderness enclaves. They identify as high-caste, mid-caste or low-caste groupings based on size (large, medium or small) but some variations of these people are of a monstrous nature, ostracised to the fringes and dark places of the world, even by the Argar.

Aroth

Aroth was the First Vampire in Scylla, and her influence was based in the nation of Sindarr. Her fol-lowers, the Servants of Aroth, believe she will rise again to reclaim her throne.

Aspiring Dream

The planned purge of Khystar people by Zealots from the Dreamlands.

Athovhar

This is the Deathless One, a revered Aystar ancestor from Kharadia, who accompanies Aidan on board the Zephyr Breeze as an observer to the ancient prophecy.

Aystar

Equivalent to Aystaran people in common fantasy settings; fair haired, golden eyed, with fast reactions and slender build. Masters of magic and operators of the airships. Tolerant of Adeni people and usually dismissive towards Argar. Mostly distant, aloof and isolationist.

Bakr

The charismatic Agar shaman who leads the So-Kech on their pilgrimage to find El-Mishra on the promises of uncovering their history to reclaim their ancestral homeland.

Baron Von-Claagen

An influential minor noble from Sindarr, leader of a contingent of Jade Talon soldiers and an associate of Lord Khannay; his outward mannerisms and pale complexion caused Aidan and his companions to suspect he was a vampire with possible connections to the Servants of Aroth.

Blue

A sentient dark blue leather-bound book that once channelled the mind and power of Velis, a powerful wizard. Blue connected with Aidan through recognition of his half-Aystar bloodline and gifts him with the ability to tap into greater magic. It no longer communicates with him, its pages now blank. Despite this, Aidan keeps it, clinging to the faint hope that the spirit of the wizard Velis, possibly an ancestor, who was freed from imprisonment but slain in Kanarzand, might one day speak to him again.

Broken Blade Inn

This is where Aidan first encounters The Observers. It is a location that attracts danger and an unwelcoming crowd, on the fringes of New Kanarzand at the edge of Gideon City.

City of Ash

This is a location referred to by Matax in Cordovar when Aidan meets him; it leads to an abandoned temple where Mhorvaeus followers known as 'The Blooded' are rumoured to be gathering.

Cordovar

An Adeni city-state, ruled by academia and famed for its colleges and libraries. Outside of Gideon City, it is the second largest civilised area on the continent of Scylla.

The Cult of the Dreaded Below

This is a dark sect within the Reaches, known for worshipping an ancient entity said to slumber in the depths of the underworld.

Dark Religion

An overarching cult of evil followers.

Deathless Ones

Revered ancestors who died in the Age of Creation but were resurrected and persist as undead advisors.

Destari

Followers of The Wasteland Druid. Nomadic, solitary and mostly incorporeal. They have become one with nature and have merged with the elements of sand and wind.

Draven Corviel

Lead Archaeologist and Expedition Leader for the New Kanarzand Bureau of Forbidden Archaeology. Specialisation: Ancient architecture and cultural anthropology. Draven's deep understanding of Khestar architectural styles and cultural practices helps decode hidden chambers in Kale Khaestas and Qualtesh. His experience with other ruins in Scylla allows him to recognise patterns that Aidan might miss.

Drazakh Khan

A monstrous Argar warlord who, during the Age of Calamity, uncovered the Dark Aethyr Shard in the Forbidden Wastes and retained it as a great symbol of his power.

El-Mishra

Once a great town, the Capital of the ancient Argarian Empire. Also known as the "Town of the Fallen Star" and said to harbour an ancient power named "The Heart of the Sands".

Elira Veylin

Arcane Historian for the New Kanarzand Bureau of Forbidden Archaeology. Specialisation: Magic-infused artefacts and arcane glyphs. Elira assists in interpreting magical runes and glyphs, including the ones on the pillar in the Chamber of Treasures. Her insights into shadow magic and Kheferu artefacts help Aidan unlock their full potential. She's fascinated by Aidan's Aethyr Mark and offers theories about its origin and significance.

Eternal Void

This is space and the wider universe in which Scylla is only one world, circling its star, Kyrathia.

Everhold

The largest nomadic Adeni settlement in the Kalos Plains.

Fallen Aystar

This is a term used to identify Aystaran people who follow the Dark Religion. They develop physical Traits, such as pale skin and dark eyes, that reveal they have chosen to follow evil.

Forbidden Wastes

This is a desolate and dangerous location in Syrnadar. It is said to be influenced by monstrous and supernatural entities from the Age of Darkness.

Gideon City

The regional Capital: a Gothic Victorian-styled city ruled by a Magocracy (The Thirteen). It is dominated by magical colleges, industry and trading guilds. Highly political and authoritarian. Policed by a guard force, overseen by The Sentinel.

Hapt-Sept Amun

A maniacal narcissistic self-made God-King, who sought immortality and summoned the power of Aethyr which cursed him and transformed him an unliving being, together with his people. Having been released from his buried city and tomb, he yearns to restore his lost Adeni.

Harvin

Captain of the Zephyr Cloud airship; a seasoned Adeni known for his sharp eye and unmatched instincts in evasive manoeuvres.

High King Iaeras I

The ruler of the Kale Khestari war clans.

House of Tyrelis

Ahlissa referenced this group as being able to assist Aidan with his deviant Aethyr Mark; but at the cost of being exploited by them for the power it may give.

Ivistar Immiar

Ahlissa is betrothed to Ivistar Immiar, a hot-headed Warlord of the Kale Khestari and a favoured warrior of High King Iaeras I. He frequently stirs conflict along the Aystaran borders, seeking to prove the honour of the Kale Khestari. Admiring Ahlissa's bold actions in Kanarzand, he tolerates Aidan but sees him as weak, often reminding him of this despite Ahlissa's scolding, which he ignores.

Izen'draazt

The Ageless One. The Dark Destroyer. The Endless Night. This ancient evil demon from the Eternal Void brings chaos to every world that it touches, bringing with it corruption and destruction. The creatures that its power touches become transformed into horrid fearsome things, colloquially known as "Unforgiven", and impervious to all ordinary weapons. There is a rare dark-red crystalline mineral pre-sent in the Tahnaar Desert that, when infused with light Aethyr and treated with the Tears of Diamh, can forge weapons that harm Izen'draazt's minions or hold them at bay.

Jillian

One of the Khystar people, a shapeshifter and the last of her kind in Syrnadar.

Kaldorin

This is the location of a small town and military staging post, built on the ruins of a ruined citadel.

Kale Ashtari

A dark natured bloodline of Khestar; Aidan fears his ancestry is linked to them.

Kale Ereshkigal

Known as the Deathless Ones, or revered ancestors, of the Aystar. They are said to be a generation re-moved from the Khestar and have been present for centuries. They are undead but are not malevolent or hostile towards living creatures.

Kale Khestari

Descended from the Khestar, these nomadic Aystaran people, a proud and intolerant warrior-caste acclimatised to long desert patrols and warfare against wild monsters and predators. Their ancestral homeland is centred on Sunhold which is located in Kharadia.

Kale Khaestas

A large desert fortress, home base of the Kale Khestari war clans.

Kanarzand

The gothic wild-western-styled frontier town in the desert, ruled by the Arcane Council (The Twelve) who have pledged allegiance to The High Magocracy (The Thirteen). Despite the semblance of authority, lawlessness is rife, and the explorer/discovery guilds have great influence because they bring the finance. Danger is every-where and both Adeni and Argar people are drawn here to seek fortune and adventure as mercenaries in the surrounding sands and ruins.

Kazum Dra

A significant region that is controlled by Argar Raiders in the Forbidden Wastes.

Keeper of the Past

A title provided to respected elders in the Temple of the Ages.

Kharadia

One of the continents that exist in the world of Scylla. It is the continent where the Aystar and Khystar people originate from.

Khestar

This was the ancient progenitor race, forefathers to the Aystar, who travelled the Eternal Void in vessels powered by Aethyr. They brought their magic and items of wondrous power to continents of Kharadia and Syrnadar when their culture spanned the globe in an Age of Enlightenment.

Kyrathia

This is the name of the star around which the planet Scylla orbits, in the Eternal Void.

Kyshtar

An ancient race that co-inhabited the world alongside the Aystar after arriving from the Eternal Void independently. Known as shapeshifters, the Adeni wizards sought to eliminate them, believing that "their kind" are dangerous for being aberrations to natural order.

Lake Glassmere

Located near the border where the Tahnaar Desert ends and the Kalos Plains begin.

Liberty Spire

This is a place frequented by the elite and wealthy of Gideon City. Ahlissa takes Aidan here one evening, after concluding his adventures with the Kale Khestari in Kharadia.

Lorian Tyraleth

A stern and accomplished war band leader. He is Aidan's martial lore tutor.

Lord Khannay

Lord Khannay was the benefactor of the library in Kanarzand and Aidan's patron. He was rumoured to be a vampire and aligned with the Servants of Aroth and Baron Von-Claagen.

Magocracy

A ruling council of wizards and magicians; in Gideon City this is The Thirteen and in Kanarzand this is The Twelve.

Malrik Fenhal

Cryptozoologist and Planar Specialist for the New Kanarzand Bureau of Forbidden Archaeology. Specialisation: Mythical creatures, planar rifts, and extra planar entities. Malrik's knowledge of extra planar entities aids in understanding the Sah'ren's presence and their connection to The Aspiring Dream. He also identifies the source of planar disturbances in Gideon and provides critical information about Izen'draazt's powers and movements.

Marthorn

This is a significant settlement and established trading post which is located in the Aethyr Reaches.

Master Brevax

Aidan's mentor. An elderly historian in Gideon City.

Matax

An agent for The Machination; he operates out of an apothecary on the eastern side of the city of Cordovar, not far from the Grand Market.

Mhargrave Outreach Society

One of the greedy archaeological factions that dominates and influences political and academic activity across all Kharadia and Syrnadar. Aidan briefly disrupts their activity when he encounters the Rogue Mercenaries at one of their dig sites in the Tahnaar Desert.

Mistress Sainar

The pragmatic and cunning Guild mistress of the Kanarzand Bureau of Forbidden Archaeology. She's an influential figure concerned about profit, knowledge control, and maintaining balance in the city. Her increasing interest in Aidan's activities marks her as a potential threat or reluctant ally.

Monks at the Temple of Twilight Calm

Ahlissa has told Aidan that this religious order may be able to help him remove the Aethyr Mark. He does not know much about them, except they offer healing in exchange for services or donations.

Oren

Oren is one of Aidan's initial companions, a former Sentinel guard from Gideon City, who leads Aidan to follow Bakr and the So-Kech to find El-Mishra. He proves himself invaluable with his quick thinking and tactical skills. His goal is to protect the desert's people from the growing darkness, fighting both external threats and the treachery of rival factions.

Ostarr

A large town at the border of Sindarr. The Citadel of Mhorvaeus is located in the hills nearby.

Queen Ashkaan

Queen Ashkaan, the iron-fisted ruler of the Argar quarter in Gideon's Old Undercity, is a towering figure of menace and mystery. Ashkaan's most defining feature is the intricately crafted metal helmet she wears at all times, a dark, spiked visage that covers her face and eyes completely. The helmet's sinister design, forged with jagged patterns and moulded to fit her head seamlessly, gives her a nightmarish, almost otherworldly appearance. It is said that the metal she chose is rare, imbued with an ancient enchantment, which she claims prevents any magic from removing it or seeing through it. Her followers believe this helmet is not merely for intimidation; Ashkaan's helmet conceals something much more terrifying beneath.

Renlor Drax

Combat Historian and Tactician for the New Kanarzand Bureau of Forbidden Archaeology. Specialisation: Historical military strategies and weaponry. Renlor's knowledge of the Final Battle at Kale Khaestas helps Aidan and the companions understand the battlefield's layout. His insights into ancient weaponry prove useful when deciphering the tactical uses of artefacts like Kheferu. Renlor also assists in planning the ambush on the Aldrosian Zealots.

Rogue Mercenaries

An Argar farmer with a lost heritage of great prestige, a mechanical creation imbued with a living soul, a low-caste Adeni priest, and a former dishonourably discharged Sentinel guard from Gideon City; this group had been gaining quite an unfortunate reputation in Kanarzand recently with their exploits and after hearing of Aidan uncovering forbidden magic (and encountering him at a Mhargrave Dig Site) they have vowed to hunt him down for bounty, on behalf of The Twelve.

Sah'ren

The vengeful spirit force that inhabits the Khystar Zealots in Aldrosia who follow the teachings of The Aspiring Dream.

Sceptre Guilds

Twelve primary houses that are aligned to particular Aethyr Marks, which in turn associate them directly with specific functions, such as trade and espionage.

Scornland

A dangerous place; destroyed by horrific magic during the Age of Calamity. The land itself is cursed. Any survivors of that cataclysm have been twisted into monsters. Healing magic doesn't work there, and the entire area is prone to violent magical storms.

Scylla

The name of the world setting for the fantasy novel; synonymous with danger.

Servants of Aroth

A fanatical cult devoted to the worship of Aroth, the First Vampire in Scylla.

Shaevath Tyrathalas

A venerable elder Keeper of the Past, and Aidan's mentor at the Temple of the Ages in Kharadia.

Silent Crescent

One of the most aggressive, clandestine and fanatical archaeological research factions; they seek ancient Khestar artefacts and are well known to Captain Ahlissa as serious competitors to her operations.

Sindarr

This is a warlike nation that aligns itself with the Dark Religion and promotes necromancy.

So-Kech

A significant religious grouping of Argar, led by a powerful Shaman named Bakr. Collectively regarded as a cult, they are also known as "Word Bearers".

Spark Rail

A train that connects Kanarzand and Gideon City across the vast expanse of the Tahnaar desert. It is magically powered and glides overland, emitting lightning around it, hence its name.

Star Haunt

This ancient, ruined place was a fortress for the Kale Ashtari, the dark bloodline of the ancient Khestar. This is where Aidan discovers his first clues and suspects his heritage may be linked to them, after his encounter with the tainted guardian.

Sunhold

The spiritual centre of knowledge and High Capital city of the Aystar people on the continent of Kharadia.

Syrnadar

One of the continents that exist in the world of Scylla. It is where the primary story locations of Gideon City and Kanarzand are located, in the middle of the Tahnaar Desert.

Tahnaar Desert

An ancient Adeni name, it was given when the three ancient empires existed.

Taint

A condition that relates to an unnatural or dark influence by something, possibly a form of possession by another entity or corruption by exposure to Dark Aethyr.

Temple of the Ages

A bastion of knowledge, its grand halls are filled with the histories and legends of the Khestar, the pro-genitors of the Aystaran people.

Tessa Lorynth

Geomancer and Sand Magic Specialist for the New Kanarzand Bureau of Forbidden Archaeology. Specialisation: Elemental magic, particularly sand-shifting techniques. Tessa's mastery of Sand Magic is invaluable in excavating buried ruins and stabilizing fragile structures. She aids in revealing new areas of Kale Khaestas and Qualtesh and helps create defensive barriers during the ambush.

Terror Lizards

Giant carnivorous reptiles that roam the Kalos Plains.

Thalendir

An ancient king of the High-Aystaran people, a direct descendant of the Khestar and Kale Khestari. His remains have a special meaning to the scattered Aystaran people.

The Blooded

This is a name given to a rumoured gathering of Mhorvaeus' followers. Aidan and Ahlissa suspect this is another name for the cult known as The Servants of Aroth.

The Glass Tower

A covert network that operates across Scylla, primarily connecting half-Aystar operatives. Their goal isn't to control Scylla, but to keep it balanced. They gather knowledge and intervene when necessary to prevent another devastating conflict like the Age of Calamity.

The Guard Post of Athosin

This is a small stone tower of Athosin, surrounded by a few modest outbuildings, which functions as an outpost for Kale Khestari warriors.

The Jade Talon

A sinister mercenary group comprised predominantly of Argar.

The Machination

An organisation that Ahlissa works for, answerable to a group called The Glass Tower.

The Observers

These three mysterious and enigmatic individuals are working for The Thirteen and are hunting for any-one who displays signs of bearing a deviant Aethyr Mark.

The Path of the Light

The faith that Aldrosian separatists uphold and preserve against the Sah'ren and The Aspiring Dream.

The Prism

This is the name given by The Glass Tower to The Zephyr Breeze, to highlight its importance as an asset to The Machination.

The Rogue Mercenaries

An unusual group causing unrest in the desert, including a dishon-ourably discharged Sentinel guard, a mechanical creation with a soul, an Argar tribesman, and a low-caste Adeni priest. They've inadvertently triggered chaos by slaughtering a nest of Zar'tul and aligning with the Mhargrave Outreach Society. After the fall of Kanarzand, the merce-naries eventually confronted Izen'draazt and defeated the monstrous entity.

The Shard of Drazakh Khan

A large dark Aethyr Shard that is protected by strange magic and requires research to unlock its secrets. Aidan believes it holds the key to answering many mysteries about the origins of Scylla.

The Thirteen

The rulers of Gideon City; The Seeker, The Gatherer, The Hunter, The Sentinel, The Maker, The Communicator, the Traveller and six others. Also known as the High Magocracy.

The Twelve

The paranoid and xenophobic rulers of Kanarzand; led by Saius, an ambitious and cruel wizard who desires control and power to rival that of The Thirteen. They wish to suppress all knowledge of any-thing that might challenge their claim to authority. Also known as the Arcane Council.

The Trust

A secret police force that operates in Cordovar that can administer strict justice without impunity or fear of reprisal.

Tiralas

A young warrior of the Kale Khestari who befriends Aidan and is a valued friend.

Velis

An ancient half-Aystar wizard that uncovered forbidden magic, result-ing in his exile and imprisonment. Through Blue, he communicates with Aidan.

Vyrethen

An Aystar advisor from the homeland in Kyrathia. Knowledgeable about the ancient Khestar.

Wasteland Druid

An ancient cursed Adeni man whose fate is tied to the Tahnaar Desert region. He masters the power of Aethyr to control the environment, bending it to his will and shaping the land. His followers are known as the Desari, or Dust Whisperers, and his power is a rival to Izen'draazt.

Wayne Scarrow

Wayne is a "Fixer" and initially presents himself as a kind benefactor on Aidan's arrival in Kanarzand. He is a manipulator who has positioned himself as a broker of information and a shrewd dealmaker, prone to outbursts of jealousy if he does not get things going his way.

Zar'tul

The sinister, demon-worshiping desert snake people who were discovered by both the academic and mercenary groups. Their extermination has upset the fragile balance with the Argar and hinted at darker forces lurking beneath the sands. There are two types of these creatures; warrior caste and shape shifters.

Zealots of Aldrosia

A generic term used to describe the fanatical Aldrosians who subscribe to the Aspiring Dream and seek to hunt down Aldrosian separatists across Scylla.

Zenot

One of the priests that accompanied the expedition to retrieve the Dark Aethyr Shard from the Under-city.

Zephyr Breeze

Captain Ahlissa's pride and joy. It operates with a mixed Adeni and Argar crew. This is one of four known Aystar magically powered vessels which also incorporate ancient Khestar technology.

Zephyr Cloud

Slightly smaller and faster than the Zephyr Breeze, this airship is often used as a scout or messenger.

Zephyr Spirit

This is a formidable airship, carrying heavier weaponry than its counterparts.

Zephyr Storm

This airship is used to conduct diplomacy, trade and other missions in the Tahnaar Desert region.

Also by Brad Williams

The Kanarzand Trilogy was produced and released between October–December 2024.
Learn more at: https://www.darkenwildepublishing.link/

KANARZAND (Book One)
Aidan, a half-Aystar scholar, becomes the target of powerful factions after awakening ancient magic linked to his heritage.

Hunted by jealous wizards, mercenaries, cultists and other adversaries, Aidan enlists the help of his new allies, including Oren, Captain Ahlissa, and Jillian, an alien shapeshifter.

Together, they embark on a dangerous journey to uncover the truth behind the hidden magic and expose the secrets of the desert.

The Dead King's Bones (Book Two)

Aidan journeys with Ahlissa and Jillian, to Sunhold, in Kharadia, to repatriate the long-lost bones of King Thalendir. In doing so, he is welcomed among the Aystar and learns about his people and their bloodlines, ultimately training as a warrior to be accepted by them.

Aidan faces new trials in the desert while, haunted by visions and terrifying nightmares, he discovers that he bears an abnormal magical mark that is associated with a dark forgotten heritage.

New threats emerge and the companions find themselves in a race against rivals to retrieve an ancient artefact from deep beneath Gideon City.

Demon Stone (Book Three)

Aidan finds himself held in the thrall of a dangerous and malevolent entity as he obsessively researches and deciphers the magic inscriptions that the Dark Aethyr Shard bears.

Aidan, Ahlissa, Jillian and their allies embark on a quest through ruins and labyrinths, uncovering secrets that link Aidan to the lost Kale Ashtari, and which lead them to rediscover the ancient lost city of Qualtesh in the Forbidden Wastes.

Demon Stone is a sweeping tale of ancient legacies, dark magic and the enduring fight for hope and unity in a fractured world.